EYES IN THE JUNGLE

EYES IN THE JUNGLE

by Bernard Palmer

MOODY PRESS

CHICAGO

TO MY DARLING DAUGHTER,

JAN

LIBRARY OF CONGRESS CATALOG CARD NUMBER 74-80945

Printed in the United States of America

Contents

Chapter   Page

1. White Teacher Arrives 7

2. Tiger Springs 16

3. Patel Believes 28

4. Patel Hides 40

5. Search Begins 52

6. Suspicion Grows 62

7. Drupadi Tells 71

8. Patel Is Found 80

9. Patel Is Punished 91

10. Drupadi Decides 101

11. Villagers Pursue 111

12. Drupadi Escapes 118

     Glossary 128

5

1

White Teacher Arrives

Drupadi stood, spreading his legs slightly, bare feet unmindful of the hard, stony ground that sloped up from the stream. He extended his slender brown arms in front of him the way he had been shown by his new American friend. He and Patel and the other boys in the mountain village of Magadi in faraway India understood about throwing stones. They could shy a rock so close to a black-faced *langur*'s head that the monkey would scream in terror and jump from tree to tree so fast that it would make them all laugh. Throwing, they could do. Catching this thing Jack Conway called a ball was something else. Drupadi didn't know if he would ever be able to do it.

The light-haired boy, who was as muscular and powerfully built as Drupadi and Patel were gaunt and arrowy, closed his stubby fingers over the ball so easily, so surely, that it seemed anyone ought to be able to do it. But when Drupadi tried, the round thing shot through his fingers and went rolling away. He spent most of his time chasing it, or so it seemed.

It had been an exciting day in Magadi when the white boy and his gaunt father came jouncing into the village from over the mountain pass. Patel had seen the dust worming up from the road against the distant sky and had given the alarm.

"Someone comes!" His shrill young voice brought heads popping out of grass-thatched huts and black eyes staring far up the dusty road at the car that was rolling down what was little more than a path. Seldom did anyone visit Magadi by car, and especially from over the mountain pass. "Someone comes!"

By the time the sturdy little jeep with no top and only a windshield in front came clattering into the square, everyone in the village had gathered in curiosity. The elders and the other men in Magadi were in the front. Drupadi and Patel and their friends were next, pressing as close as they dared in order to hear what these strangers had to say. And the women and little children lurked on the outer rim of the tense group, curious but fearful.

Drupadi's gaze sharpened as he saw the driver of the vehicle. He had heard his father, Mukerji, tell about the white-skinned ones who used to come to the village, but that had been many years before. He had never once supposed that he would see them with his own two eyes. But here they were, two of them.

The thin muscles in Drupadi's jaw tightened as the fair-skinned giant behind the wheel unhinged himself and climbed out beside Sacuni, the village's wise and powerful leader. Drupadi had never seen anyone so tall and with such broad shoulders. This stranger was almost as big as a *niagroda* tree. He seemed as big as a sacred cow among the goats, as an elephant towering above his *mahout* or handler. *It would not be good to get a clout from that fist,* he reasoned.

Slowly Drupadi's attention focused on the younger one. He was a boy like himself, although heavier and with hair almost as white as his skin, and eyes that looked like bits of sky. But he was about Drupadi's height, and the smile on his lips whispered that he wanted to be friends.

At first Drupadi was not sure he dared to be friends with them. They might be gods sent by the messenger of spirits, Narada. And to make friends with gods could only make trouble. But the more he thought about it, the more sure he was that they must be men like the villagers. His father had told him about such people who used to come to Magadi many years ago. He called them men, and so it must be. His father was an elder in the village and wise in the things of the spirits.

While the big man talked with Sacuni and the other village leaders, his son saw that Drupadi was eyeing him. He started in his direction, his smile widening. Terrified that one of the strangers would single him out, the Indian boy would have whirled and fled but the press of the crowd held him captive. A dull red stain climbed to his cheeks and fear sparked cold flames in his eyes as he saw the stranger move toward him.

"Greetings," the white one said in the language of the people.

He talked funny, Drupadi noticed, saying the words in a strange way, as though he wasn't always sure just how he should say them. But Drupadi could understand him, he had to admit.

"Greetings."

The dark-skinned lad placed the palms of his hands together, fingers pointing toward the tip of his nose, and bowed slightly from the waist. This was the greeting of respect and not that of one boy to another. But Drupadi was bewildered and still a bit frightened. He wasn't sure just how he should speak to this one who was so different from him.

"I am named Jack," the stranger said. "Jack Conway."

Jack. The word was unfamiliar on Drupadi's tongue, but it had a pleasant sound. He would have liked to try to say it, but he did not quite dare.

"And what is your name?"

He hesitated. He had been so confused by the stranger and the fact that he had chosen to talk to him that he had not even thought the one called Jack would want to know his name.

"I am named Drupadi."

"Greetings," Jack said once more. Only this time he held out his hand in a strange way. "Greetings, Drupadi."

Drupadi backed off, almost involuntarily, until he bumped the person behind him and could go no farther.

"This is the way we greet each other in the land where I live." Jack took his hand and shook it vigorously.

That was a strange greeting, the Indian boy thought. It might be all right for one boy to greet another in such a manner, but it seemed not to show the proper respect for an elder or some esteemed stranger. He would have liked to ask this one called Jack about that, but of course it would not have been polite; and one was always courteous and considerate of those who were guests in the village.

Patel pushed forward and spoke to the stranger. He was not like Drupadi but was as bold as the *shere,* the tiger. There was no fear in his eyes as he talked to Jack.

"I was the one who saw you first," he boasted. "I saw the dust on the road that leads down from the mountain pass and shouted so everyone could hear me."

Patel was so loud and such a braggart that Drupadi was ashamed for him.

But Jack did not seem to notice. "It was a long, hard pull over the mountain from Chalama," he said.

Patel's gaze met his brazenly. "Why do you come to Magadi?" he demanded.

Drupadi's eyes flashed quickly in Jack's direction, expecting him to take offense at Patel's rudeness. Again he was ashamed for his friend. A proper Indian boy was more considerate—more respectful. But this still did not disturb the stranger; he acted as though Patel had every right to question him.

"My father is talking to your elders about coming to teach in your village."

Drupadi's slim body jerked erect. They knew about teaching. The old and wise ones in the village were careful to teach those who were young. They taught the ways of their people, about the gods and the spirits, and about making sacrifices and prayers in the Temple of Rocks. But what could these whose skin was white and who had never before been to Magadi know of such things?

Patel's black eyes slitted questioningly. "What is this—this teaching you come to do?"

"My father wants to tell your people about God," Jack said simply.

This was even more strange to Drupadi. They already had their gods and the spirits of the unseen world. There were the sacred cows and the king of the snakes, Tacsaca, and Kali, the evil spirit. Why did they need to hear about another god?

All of this Drupadi considered in his mind without speaking out loud. He would not have this Jack Conway know his secret thoughts. Already he had a good feeling toward this stranger; he was one he would like to have for a friend.

Of course the elders would never let the tall one come and tell about this strange God, he reasoned. He had heard his father say that those who didn't go to the Temple of Rocks to worship only confused the people. And, somehow, he had the feeling this white teacher would not go there to sacrifice and pray. If the elders would not allow Sahib Conway to teach in Magadi, he and his son would not come across the mountain again to visit the village. That knowledge brought great sorrow to Drupadi. He liked this one called Jack and longed to know him better.

After a time the tall one turned to his smaller companion and spoke in some strange way that caused Drupadi's lower jaw to sag in astonishment. Never had he heard such words! Nobody could know what such talking meant. But Jack seemed to understand. At least he answered in the same way. Then he turned back to Drupadi and Patel and spoke in a proper language.

"My father says it is time to go now."

Patel stuck his dark fist into Jack's as though he had been making such greetings all his life. Drupadi would have liked to do the same, but he had not the courage for it. He was afraid of what the stranger would think.

"You will come back?" he managed as their new friend climbed into the jeep. His voice sounded dry and taut, as though it belonged to some frog far from the water, and was not his at all.

"We will be back to get the answer of the elders."

Drupadi and Patel watched as the jeep wheeled about and headed back in the direction it had come. The vehicle slowed as it met a lumbering oxcart, turned out for it, and went roaring on with the noise of a hundred lowing buffaloes. A minute or two later all that could be seen was the thin, twisting spiral of dust spewing up behind the vehicle. The villagers continued to talk wonderingly for a time.

"They will never let them come back," Drupadi said to

Patel, making no attempt to hide his disappointment from his best friend. "The elders will never let them come back to teach of another god."

"Maybe they will," Patel said hopefully. "There are those who like to hear new things."

That was the way Patel was. Everything was going to work out all right; there couldn't be any other way. There was no need for concern—no need for worry. Everything would work out for the best.

Once the jeep was out of sight Drupadi made his way back to the mud hut he shared with the rest of the family. Theirs was one of the smaller houses in the village, with walls of bamboo sticks standing perpendicular to the ground, and a grass-thatched roof. There was only an opening for an entrance; no door barred the chill of the mountain nights. There was a smaller opening high up from the ground on the opposite wall. It served to let in light and air.

The family was poor, but they were Brahmin, and Mukerji, his father, was highly regarded by everyone. Sacuni often sought his counsel.

Inside, Mukerji was voicing his concern at what had happened in the village that afternoon. He was disturbed, as Drupadi knew he would be.

"Sacuni and the others want to let this stranger—this—this Sahib Conway come back to Magadi to talk with the people about his God."

Drupadi listened quietly. He dare not let his father know how this information kindled hope in his heart.

"They say it is a great honor for our village to have a vehicle come regularly over the mountain. They say that if we let him teach, some of us might be able to ride with him sometime, or we might have things brought to us from Chalama."

What they were saying was true. Drupadi knew that his own pulse beat even more rapidly in the hollow of his throat as he saw the jeep bounce away. He, too, would give much to ride in it.

"What the sahib said was pleasant to the ears, my father," Kittu murmured respectfully.

Drupadi saw that, like himself, his older brother hoped the elders would let this white stranger come back to the village to teach.

Fear contorted their father's dark face. "He will only confuse our people and bring shame to our village!" he retorted balefully. "He will bring the vengeance of the gods upon us."

Drupadi shuddered. He had heard much about the vengeance of the gods. Let someone die of the bite of a sacred cobra or of the sickness that made the stomach bloat, and his father would say it was because the gods were angry. And when the gods were angry and called for vengeance, it was so. It had to be. There was no turning them away from it.

"They will talk again tomorrow," Mukerji said, bony fingers nervously seeking the beads about his neck. "I have warned them, but they will not listen to me."

"You think they will let him come back to teach, my father?" Drupadi asked, trying to make it sound as though he was only curious and didn't really care one way or the other.

"I have warned them," his father repeated. "But they will decide to let him come when they meet tomorrow." The tone in his voice was that of dread. "And it is not good—it is not good."

Drupadi was so anxious that the sahib be permitted to come back and teach in the village that he was sure the elders would not allow it. Such a good thing could not happen to him; it could not happen to Magadi. His father and Patel would be proved wrong. The elders would think on the matter throughout the night and the next morning they would decide that this stranger should not be allowed to return to teach and risk stirring up the people and bringing shame upon them all.

But they did return! And everyone in the village had come to listen. Everyone, that is, except Mukerji and a few of his admirers. They held out against it.

"We, alone, shall be spared the calamity that is to befall Magadi because of this thing the elders are permitting," Mukerji said at home. Suspicion shone from his black eyes as he focused on his oldest sons, Kittu and Drupadi. "You are not to go near the place where this white man is teaching. Do you understand?"

"Yes, my father," Kittu retorted quickly. A little too quickly, it seemed to Drupadi, as though he spoke so because he wanted to convince their father, and not because he agreed with him in his own heart.

"I will not go to listen to the sahib's talk of this strange God either," Drupadi promised.

Their father nodded his approval. "The gods have given me good sons. May you both come back to earth in your next incarnation in pleasant, happy forms."

2

Tiger Springs

Drupadi had promised his father that he would not go to the square and listen to the teacher, but Mukerji had said nothing to him about not making friends with the teacher's son, Jack. That was the thing that interested Drupadi more than hearing what the sahib would say about this new God.

He and Patel waited with growing impatience from one visit to the next for the white boy to return. Patel would meet Jack boldly in the square, shoving through the crowd to the side of the jeep. He acted as though he didn't care who saw him as he stuck out his bony fingers to greet their new friend.

Drupadi longed to do as Patel did, but that was not possible. He always found a good reason for not going with him to meet Jack in the village. He either had to run an errand for his father, or mind the baby while his mother went to the marketplace, or help Kittu with the goats for just a little while.

"Should we play catch at the stream today?" he would ask Patel. "I'll meet you there as soon as I finish what I have to do."

Or he would meet Patel and Jack on the other side of the grove where no one ever went and there was little danger of being seen. He tried hard to keep the two boys from know-

16

ing the real reason why he did not walk out of the village with them. There were times when he was afraid they would guess the truth, but neither of them said anything, so he felt he must have been successful in keeping them from knowing his secret. But, successful or not, he could not risk having his father know whom he was with. That would take more courage than he had.

It was fun talking with the son of the teacher. Jack told them strange and wonderful things about the land of his home—things that they only half believed. He told them about roads that did not get muddy during the wet season or dusty in the dry season, about houses that got neither hot nor cold inside, and about water that was brought into the houses in hollow pieces of iron like bamboo or the barrel of a rifle. He told them about lights that hung from the ceiling that made the inside of the house as bright as day, even in the middle of the night when the moon was down and no stars were shining, and of boxes for meat that got so cold they would freeze anything that was put inside.

Both boys longed to see that marvelous land across the sea and they talked often about it.

But a change was coming over Patel that Drupadi could not help noting. He would stay with Jack and Drupadi while the teacher was visiting in the homes where he was welcome. But when the time came for the sahib to give the lesson using a cloth board and little pictures of people, Patel would leave them abruptly, regardless of what they were doing, and head back to the village.

"I have to hear what happens next," he explained.

Now and then Drupadi made his way cautiously back to the village, slipping among the shadows to a spot where he could hear and see without the risk of being seen. He wished he could be like his friend and not care who saw him

there, but Patel did not have Mukerji as his father. Patel's
father, Nala, did not seem to care what he did.

Drupadi would not soon forget the afternoon when his
brother Kittu had come to him with the dread news that
he knew Drupadi had been listening to the teacher. Kittu
had glared ominously down at him, face dark with fury.

* * *

"Drupadi!" Kittu's voice was a hoarse whisper. "You
have been going to hear that teacher after our father
warned you against it!"

The younger boy started, cheeks fading. His brother had
found out he was in the square when the teacher was
speaking. Somehow he knew. *He knew!*

"Who told you I was there?"

"Don't try to lie to me. I saw you hiding in the shadows!"

Dismay flamed beneath Drupadi's drooping eyelids and
he jerked a quick breath into his lungs between slightly
parted lips. And he had been so sure he had been careful in
approaching the crowd around the teacher! So sure he
wouldn't be seen!

"You dare not tell our father!" Drupadi retorted. "You
were there yourself, last week." He made no open threat—
just the reminder that he knew about Kittu as well. He saw
his brother flinch at the news. That would be enough to
check his older brother's careless tongue.

"I won't have to tell him," Kittu hissed when he recov-
ered from the news that he had been seen listening to the
teacher. "Someone else will do it for me. You have heard
the talk in the village. You know what our father and some
of the others are saying."

"They talk so only because they do not know the teacher
the way we know him," Drupadi said, speaking guardedly

but with a passion he did not know he felt. "There is only kindness in his heart."

Kittu drew himself erect haughtily, burning with pride. "He is not one of us," he lashed out. "You see the color of his skin. And they say he teaches the untouchables!" His lips curled scornfully about the word as though it were an epithet. "It is said he has them in his house at Chamala across the mountains, and that he goes to their huts to visit them." He stopped indignantly. "And *you* would listen to such a one as that!"

"It is *said!*" Drupadi spat out the scalding words as though they blistered his tongue. "It is *said!* Tell me, Kittu, were you there? Did you see it with your own two eyes? Can you swear that he does those things?" It was hard for Drupadi to believe that Sahib Conway would befriend the lower-caste untouchables whose touch could defile high-caste Brahmins.

Arrogance ran its angry fingers over the older boy's face. "Our father said that one of the elders asked him about it, and he did not deny it."

Drupadi weighed that bit of information thoughtfully. There might be something to what Kittu was saying. This teacher thought for himself and did as he believed to be right. He was not the same as others the boy knew.

"I know not about the untouchables, my brother," he admitted after a time. "Maybe it happens. Maybe it does not happen. But this I do know. The words of the teacher about this One called Jesus bring joy to my heart."

Kittu gasped at the blasphemy. "Do not talk that way! I know that of which you are speaking. As he talked this afternoon, my heart was aflame within me and I found myself longing to know more about this One who the Sahib Conway says loves us so very much. But, Drupadi, we dare not listen!" His voice caught significantly, as though the words were too awful for him to utter.

A question wrinkled the younger boy's serious face. "Why does our father say we should put it aside, Kittu?" he asked. "It is not evil the sahib speaks about. It is good."

His older brother spat contemptuously on the ground. "Good?" he demanded. "Would it be good to face our father with the news that either you or I had forsaken our people's gods and was walking the way of the teacher's new God?"

Drupadi shuddered. It was thinking about such things that kept him awake in the dark of the night when the rest of the family was sleeping. It was such things that made him so fearful he could not think.

"Would it be good to be called before the elders and have them decide that we should be stoned?"

Drupadi blanched. Such things were enough to steal the heart of anyone.

"You talk as though I, too, am a follower of the Jesus-way," Drupadi protested with growing fervency. "You talk that way because I have gone to hear what the sahib has to say and because I like to play with this thing called a ball that his son, Jack, brings with him."

Desperation kindled in his older brother's eyes and burned deep as he moved closer. "I can see what is happening to you!" he muttered darkly. "That is why I talk to you now. So I can warn you!"

"You can see nothing!" Drupadi was suddenly angry. "You know nothing!"

"I see your face and the lights that glow there while the teacher talks," Kittu reminded him.

"The same lights I see in yours?" the younger one taunted.

Kittu cuffed him savagely with the back of his hand. Drupadi stumbled backward and almost fell.

"I am warning you, Drupadi! Go hear the missionary one more time and our father will know of it! That I promise you!"

Drupadi slunk away from his older brother, still rubbing the tender spot on his cheek where he had been struck. He knew well enough that Kittu meant everything that he had said. If he went to hear the teacher once more, their father would learn of it. And there was nothing he could do about it. It was enough to make one die inside.

At the evening meal when the family was all together that night, Mukerji could speak of but little else than this white stranger who had come from across the mountain ridge to teach the people about a new God.

"Nothing good can come of it," he said solemnly. "He will have all the village in an uproar."

"Yes, my father," Kittu agreed.

"Old Drona learned that his three sons had gone to hear the white man and he beat them until he broke his club. They will not soon disobey in that way again."

Drupadi found sudden interest in his food, but he was scarcely aware of what he was eating.

"I hope my two sons are wise enough to keep the white man's words from tickling their ears."

"I never go there," Kittu said quickly. "I have no wish to hear of foreign gods. The gods of our people are the gods for me. I wish they would not let this sahib come to Magadi to teach; he only confuses people with his words."

"I do not go to hear him either," Drupadi lied. He knew this Jesus would not have been pleased to hear him speak untruths, but that was better than facing his father's anger. He *knew* what that would be!

After that Drupadi was careful not to listen to Sahib Conway and was even more careful than before to avoid being seen in the company of the teacher's son. They always met someplace away from Kittu's prying eyes and those of others who might carry the news back to Mukerji.

From time to time when they were fooling around on the far side of the grove or along the stream Jack tried to get him to go back into the village in time to hear the lesson. He tried again that afternoon.

Again the Indian boy refused firmly. "Let's play catch."

Jack Conway didn't act as though he wanted to play ball that afternoon, but he fished it out of his pocket.

"All right. You go down there." He motioned along the bank of the stream. "I'll stay here."

Drupadi did as he was told, glad to have the problem of listening to the lesson solved for another week.

"You remember how to hold your hands, don't you?"

Drupadi put them up in front of him. "So?"

"That's fine."

Jack threw the ball. He didn't throw it hard and he sent it as straight as he could. Drupadi was sure he was going to catch it this time. He judged it correctly as it came toward him and met it with his hands. But it ticked his fingers and bounded away from him down the slope in the direction of the stream. He leaped after it, stopping it on the very edge of the water. His fingers were closing over the smooth surface when he froze motionless, as though he had been suddenly cast in bronze.

He stared at the strange imprint in the sand.

"Come on, Drupadi!" his companion called out impatiently. "If we're going to play catch, let's get with it."

Drupadi's lips parted, but no sound came out. He had never seen tracks like those before, but he knew what they

were. His father had traced one for him in the sand.

"This is the pad—so," Mukerji had explained. "And here are the toes. When you see this pug mark, Drupadi, you know to run quick!"

By this time Jack saw that something was wrong and came over to him curiously.

"What is it, Drupadi?"

The boy pointed, his throat suddenly robbed of words.

"Looks like the track of some big cat," Jack said aloud.

The Indian boy's gaze met his, black eyes staring behind heavy, squinting lids. *"Shere!"* he managed to whisper tensely. "Tiger!"

Jack pulled in his breath sharply.

Drupadi straightened with difficulty and looked about, half expecting the dread *shere* to come pouncing out of the shadows to devour them. He knew what his father and his father's friends would be saying when they heard of the visit of the dread tiger to their area. They would be muttering that Narada, the messenger of spirits, had sent the tiger to punish the village for letting the teacher come to Magadi and tell the people about this new God. And they would prophesy darkly that Iama, the spirit of death, would not be far behind.

It brought fear to Drupadi just to think about what they would be saying.

But there was no time to think about the fear the danger-ous *shere* would bring to Magadi. Even now the tiger might be stalking him and Jack, moving stealthily through the bush, gaunt sides blending into the pattern of leaves and branches until he was unseen. He might be lurking out there anywhere, great ugly eyes fixed on Drupadi and his companion, seeking to destroy them.

Drupadi's head came up, sudden fear glittering in his eyes. He wanted to turn and flee, but he could not. Some-thing he did not quite understand held him there forcibly.

Drupadi stared back at the great pug marks. He wished he could read them as well as his father and Kittu could. They could examine such tracks in the sand so skillfully that they could tell how long it had been since the tiger passed that way. Sometimes they could tell if he was hungry and hunting, or going down to the stream to drink, or just passing through. There were many things they could read in a few faint tracks. All Drupadi knew, however, was that the fearful animal must be huge because he had left such tremendous pug marks in the sand.

He studied the tracks with care. Now that he looked closely, there were other things he could tell by them—things he had only dimly been aware of before. The tiger had walked along the stream, stopping here to drink. And he must have been hungry. The tracks went off in one direction a few paces and then came back, as though he had been searching for food. Or, he might have had another purpose. The thought chilled Drupadi. Maybe the tiger had been looking for him, or Patel, or one of the women who came to the stream for water. He might have come to wreak the vengeance of the gods on the village.

Drupadi's heart almost stopped.

Jack hunkered beside him. "Are they really tiger tracks?" he asked uncertainly, as though such a thing could not be.

Drupadi did not answer him. He knew that Jack had lived in the high country of India most of his life. He knew that his companion was well aware that of all the game in that vast country only the tiger, the hated and feared *shere,* could leave such marks in the sand.

Shock had forced the question from Jack—shock and the vague hope that somehow both he and Drupadi could be wrong. Jack was trying to convince himself that those tracks meant nothing at all.

The youthful Indian was well aware of this because he had to fight the same yearning himself. He yearned to pretend that the pug marks didn't exist, or that they had been made by some lesser creature. But that did not change the truth that those tracks had been left there by the tiger and only the tiger.

"What are we going to do?" Jack asked, his voice flat and shaken. In playing catch he was the authority, constantly telling Drupadi how to hold his hands and how to judge the ball so he could be in the right position when it reached him. Now, however, he turned instinctively to his Indian companion. "What should we do?"

"We'll have to get back to the village first, and tell the people," Drupadi replied. "Then—"

His voice choked into silence. Then there would be a great stir. The oldest and wisest hunters would gather the men and older boys together and lead them out on the mountain in search of the dreaded *shere*. There were no guns in Magadi. It would be better if there were, although only two or three knew how to shoot them. All they had for weapons were their short spears and clubs. Fear would make their mouths dry and coppery and cause their legs to tremble, but they would go because they had to. It was the only way of ridding the village of this grave danger.

If the gods were with them, they would come back triumphantly, carrying the tiger with his legs tied over a pole to the center of the village for all to see. There would be feasting and rejoicing. More likely, they would come dragging wearily back at night, their bodies trembling on the edge of exhaustion, and their fear like so many stones in the bottom of their stomachs. And the women would continue to keep the children in their houses, and would even be afraid to go out to the streams for water.

Then the talk would begin. At first it would be in guarded whispers, passing from one frightened ear to another. But each would add to it, building the story bigger and more frightening.

Could it be that this was a visit sent by the gods because of the white sahib and the things he was teaching? Could it be that the village was singled out for a special curse? Those questions and more would pass from one quaking villager to the other, who would be concerned that even the speaking of those things might be enough to bring them to pass.

Drupadi knew what his father would say. He, and a few

of those he had been able to influence, opposed the teacher's coming to Magadi from the beginning. He would be determined to set the people against the white man and his son until they could no longer come to the village. Or—Drupadi shuddered at the thought—Mukerji might decide that striking against Sahib Conway and his son would appease the gods and cause them to withdraw the curse.

That could not be, he tried to tell himself. His father was stern and demanding; all good fathers were. But there were kindness and gentleness there. They softened his eyes and the lines in his face. He was not one who would enjoy bringing harm to the strangers. But because he was so frightened by what had already happened, he probably would be terrified at the presence of the tiger on the mountain slope near Magadi.

Drupadi had to admit that he, too, was fearful when he thought about the *shere* and the possibility that he was there to avenge the gods. The things the missionary said were pleasant to the ear and warm to the stomach, but the spirits could not be pushed aside so easily. And now that the tiger had appeared, Drupadi was more bewildered and confused than ever.

3

Patel Believes

Drupadi turned hurriedly and started in the direction of the village. Jack had been struck silent by the sight of the tiger's pug marks; but now that they were rushing to Magadi, his tongue loosened.

"What will the people do when you tell them about the tiger, Drupadi?" he asked. "Will they go out after him? Will they try to kill him before he hurts anyone?"

Drupadi nodded without breaking stride.

"Do you suppose we could go along?" Excitement and anticipation filled Jack's voice.

Drupadi had no answer. To go would be exciting, it was true. The thought caught hold of him in much the same way as it caught hold of his companion. But there were things Jack did not know. There would be no guns—only spears and such clubs as the men could find or make. If they should corner the *shere* and he pounced on them, ugly fangs flashing, before they could drive a spearhead into a vital spot— It was a fearful thing.

"My father has a gun," Jack announced, as though he sensed what his Indian companion was thinking. "He will come and help kill the tiger if they want him to."

A gun? Drupadi's heart leaped. With a gun the *shere* would not be so terrible. He could be tracked down and shot. One bullet in the right place and—pouf—the tiger would never bother anyone else again.

28

"We will talk to him first," Drupadi said.

It would be better to get the consent of the sahib to go on the hunt with them before the people knew about the tiger. Perhaps that would keep them from getting so frightened and so angry with the white man and his son.

Drupadi hurried on, his mind racing as rapidly as his bony legs. Maybe this God the sahib told about was stronger than the gods of the villagers, he reasoned. Maybe He knew about the curse even before it happened, and provided the teacher with a rifle to destroy the tiger and overcome Kali's plan for vengeance. It didn't seem possible that the teacher's God could be more powerful than the evil spirit, Kali, but the sahib talked as if he believed it to be true.

So concerned was Drupadi about the tiger's pug marks along the stream that he forgot to be careful not to be seen with the teacher's son. Together they ran through the village to the square where the white man was giving the lesson.

At the fringe of the crowd they stopped uncertainly. Drupadi would have broken in at once, so important did he believe the news of the tiger to be, but Jack laid a hand on his arm.

"My father is almost finished," he whispered. "We'll wait until he is through. OK?"

The Indian boy agreed reluctantly.

Kittu came up to him while they waited. "Where have you been?" he demanded.

Drupadi eyed him uncomfortably. "Out along the stream," he said, "looking for stones."

"Our father was here looking for you," Kittu whispered. "He can't be more than a hundred paces away right now."

Drupadi's eyes rounded and his gaze darted quickly over

the crowd, suddenly frantic that someone there would tell Mukerji that his sons were in the group that was listening to the strange teacher.

"He is afraid you are being swayed from the ways of our people by this new teaching," his older brother said. "He came to look for you, to see if you are coming here against his wishes."

Drupadi's lithe body stiffened. So his father was suspicious! Somebody must have seen him playing ball with the teacher's son and had told Mukerji. Fear swept up his spine in great, chilling spasms. He could lie to his father. He had done it often enough before when it suited his purpose. But Mukerji had an uncanny way about him when it came to ferreting out the truth.

"I—" Drupadi began.

But at that instant Patel, who had been standing some distance away listening intently to the teacher, spoke up with a firm, clear voice.

"Sahib!"

It came so suddenly it startled Conway as well as the villagers who were listening. Heads snapped around, eyes focusing on the bold lad who stood among them.

"Yes?"

Drupadi wanted to dash through the crowd, grab Patel by the arm and jerk him away before he had time to get himself into more trouble than he was in already. But Drupadi stood numbly like everyone else—stunned by this new development.

"This Jesus you tell about," Patel went on, unmindful of the fact that all the village was listening. "I would be His follower, Sahib! I would walk with Him!"

Drupadi caught his breath. That Patel! Didn't he know what would happen to him now? Had he gone out of his mind? But his friend shouldered his way through the crowd to stand beside the tall white teacher.

Kittu poked his brother in the side with a bony finger. "When our father hears what Patel, your good friend, has done," he whispered, "he is going to be more suspicious than ever about you, my brother."

Drupadi scowled. "I am not Patel's shadow," he retorted irritably. "I do not follow him everywhere he goes and do all that he does. He speaks for himself."

"You do not have to convince me," his older brother told him. "It is our father who will be questioning."

The younger boy's temper flamed. But even as his face flushed, he realized that Kittu had only spoken the truth. Their father was already suspicious and questioning. When he heard of what Patel had done—and he would be among the first to hear it. He always was among the first to know everything that went on in the village. When he heard what Patel had done it would be difficult, indeed, for Drupadi to convince him that he, too, was not making the same decision.

The slender Indian lad jerked himself erect. How could he tell his father or anyone else about the tracks of the *shere* now? If he did, Mukerji would soon learn that the Sahib's son was with him. And with his closest friend now walking the Jesus way, Drupadi would never be able to convince his father that he, too, was not turning his back on the old ways.

He trembled convulsively. What could he do? What should he do? Silently he turned and blended into the shadows. Why did Patel have to be so foolish as to speak out openly? He could not understand that. It was true that the things Sahib Conway said brought a warm glow to his heart and made him long to hear more. Patel, too, had found his words so. But why did he have to speak out so plainly? No one could have looked into his mind!

Why hadn't Patel clung to those things deep inside where no one could know about it? Why hadn't he let those who were so bitter against this Jesus think he still believed the same as his father and his father's fathers? He did not have to speak out the way he did.

When Drupadi got home his father was waiting for him, dismay and anger creasing the harsh lines of his dark face.

"Where have you been?" Mukerji grated harshly.

In that instant the boy knew that his father had already heard about Patel. He knew he would have to say something, that he would have to make an explanation, but for the moment he could not speak.

"What have you been doing?"

Drupadi cleared his throat with a nervous cough. "Down by the stream, gathering stones," he said defensively.

"You were with Patel," his father said accusingly, half statement of fact, half question.

"Not since yesterday was I with him." Drupadi was so frightened that it was only with difficulty that he could speak.

"You say the truth?" Doubt still glittered in his father's narrowing eyes.

"I say the truth, my father," Drupadi replied, his voice trembling.

Mukerji searched his son's face, wanting to believe him but not knowing if he dared. "You weren't with Patel, then?"

The frightened boy took no offense at his father's persistent questioning. He had to convince him that he was not with his friend that day and that he had not been listening to the accursed message of the teacher. He had to convince him of it himself so that his father would not talk with anyone else about it, and so he would not go about asking questions of those who were in the square when the teacher spoke. That was the only way Drupadi could keep him from knowing that he had spent the afternoon with the teacher's son.

"Yesterday I was only with him for a little while," he said. "Today I was not with him at all."

His father leaned forward, eyes gleaming angrily as his gaze bore into the very depths of Drupadi's being.

"If I find you lied to me, my son—" The threat did not have to be voiced. They both knew that such a development would go hard with Drupadi.

"He wasn't with Patel," Kittu broke in. "I saw Patel myself before the white man talked. He wasn't with anyone; he was alone."

Mukerji's gaze snapped to one side to stare into the face of his firstborn son.

"And how do you know that?" he rasped. "Were you there, listening to this teacher of lies?"

Kittu's eyes did not waver. "Would I dare to tell you that I saw Patel if I had been there listening?" he asked. "Especially after what happened in the square today?"

That seemed to satisfy the concerned Mukerji that neither of his sons had been at the meeting where Patel had disgraced himself and his family. The muscles in their father's face relaxed slightly and a thin, wispy smile kissed his lips for an instant. He nodded gravely.

"You are right, Kittu. Only a fool would do so." He fingered the beads about his neck, as though drawing strength from them. "Long have I asked the gods to give me sons a man can take pride in—sons who will hold our

fathers' ways close to their hearts, sons who will not offend
the sacred cow or the cobra and who will be respectful to
Narada, the messenger of spirits. That kind of son would
not go chasing off after this new religion the white teacher
speaks about; he would not bring shame upon the head of
his father."

Drupadi eyed Kittu gratefully. He had been surprised
when his brother spoke up for him.

"Patel is a fool!" Mukerji repeated. His lips curled. "He
will make his father, Nala, the laughingstock of our village.
He will bring shame upon all his family and send them to
their graves in disgrace."

Drupadi fell silent. He wanted to know what the elders
were saying about Patel and what they planned to do to
him, but he had only narrowly avoided discovery. He dared
not show his interest yet. Such concern would only light the
fires under his father's fears once more and make him doubt
that his younger son had told the truth. It was better to
remain silent although his thoughts were continually on his
friend.

At last Kittu gave voice to the words Drupadi longed to
speak. "What do the elders say about Patel?" he asked.
"What will they do to him, my father?"

Mukerji spoke thoughtfully. "Tomorrow the matter will
be considered," he said. "They have asked Nala to appear
before them."

Drupadi did not know what the elders would do but, as
far as he could see, it meant only bad trouble for his
friend.

As the others fell silent, Drupadi resisted the desire to
leave the hut immediately and seek out his friend. If he
could just make Patel understand how dangerous it was for
him to take such a stand alone—how important it was that

he turn his back on this strange God before it was too late.

But he dared not leave. So agitated was his father that the slightest hint that he was going to contact Patel could bring great trouble to himself. And so, all he could do was to sit at home as though nothing had happened, although his soul was burning.

That night they went to bed at the same time as usual, rolling out their mats, one against the other, on the floor.

But sleep was not for Drupadi. Somewhere out on the mountain slope was the hated *shere,* the beautiful, wicked tiger who watered the courage of even the bravest men. The tracks were there for anyone to see along the bank of the stream, but few people found their way to that remote spot. It might be weeks before anyone would happen upon them, and by then it might be too late.

He ought to waken his father even now and tell him about the tiger so the rest of the village could be warned and there would be a chance of destroying the dangerous beast before he killed someone.

It would have been hard enough for Drupadi to have told his father when he first came back that afternoon. He had been afraid to tell him then, but now it would be even worse. If his father learned the truth, he would believe Drupadi was walking in Patel's footsteps; and nothing his son could say would change him.

He lay there, eyes wide and staring, miserably longing for the morning. There was nothing he could do. There was nothing he *dared* to do.

And his friend Patel had spoken out boldly before all the village. "Sahib, I would follow this Jesus!"

If only he had such courage! But he did not. So he rolled

and turned uneasily, still trying to wish the grim, tortured night away.

The next morning he could contain himself no longer. He was out of the hut as soon as they finished the morning meal, looking for his friend. He would have gone to Patel's hut directly. It was not far away. But as he turned in that direction he saw old Sacuni peering at him through sunken, watery eyes. His fleeting courage vanished and he hurried up a different path, shame hot on his cheeks.

He casually asked a few questions about his friend—the sort of questions anyone might ask. Nobody had seen Patel since the afternoon before when he spoke out so shockingly in the square. And with good reason, declared those whom Drupadi asked. There were those who prophesied that Patel would never again be seen in Magadi. Others said his mind would be stolen from him. Still others expected Nala to beat his son until Iama, the spirit of death, came and took him away.

"But it is better than having a disbelieving son," one of the old ones said. "The only way Nala can cause the gods to look with favor upon his family again is to punish Patel in the way the gods direct."

Listening to them was almost more than Drupadi could bear. But he had to act as though such treatment would be just and proper, even for one as close to him as Patel. He could not have those men planting doubts in his father's mind about his own loyalty. Although Drupadi burned to find out what the elders and Nala had adjudged to be proper punishment for his friend, it was not until that night at home that he learned what had taken place.

"The council talked with the father of this friend of yours, my son," Mukerji intoned solemnly. "He told us that he talked with Patel last night and his son says he will no longer walk the way of this strange God."

Disbelief flamed in the boy's eyes. He had been there and had heard Patel's ringing declaration. It came from a persuaded mind and a changed heart, he was sure. That Patel would turn so quickly was unthinkable. Disappointment crept in to trouble the Indian lad.

But then he remembered that he himself had planned to convince Patel to do that very thing.

For no matter how inviting the teacher's words sounded, the old ways of their people were the best for them. And they were the only way for Patel; any other course would be disastrous.

"It is good that Nala's firstborn son decided to turn his back on this strange God," Mukerji continued. "If he did not, he could disrupt the entire village and bring dishonor to all of us."

"Yes, my father," Kittu agreed dutifully.

Drupadi glanced quickly at him, his anger growing. It was one thing to keep silent because of fear for what their father might do. It was another to pretend as though he hated Sahib Conway and the words he spoke, when he, too, had heard with gladness.

Drupadi asked his father if it was all right for him to be friends with Patel again. Not that he planned to follow his father's pronouncement in the matter; he only wanted to learn how careful he would have to be to avoid being seen and getting into trouble himself.

"Patel has purged himself of blame," Mukerji said. "It is good that you show yourself to be his friend now so he will see that he did right in rejecting this new God."

Drupadi had not quite expected such openness. But that only showed his father's love and understanding for those who walked in the paths of their people.

The following morning Drupadi sought out Patel. His
friend was sitting near the thatched hut, eyes vacant and
staring as he approached. For one tortured moment he
feared that Nala had done something to his son to steal his
mind, but his friend saw him and spoke. Drupadi sat down
beside him.

"My father told me you have turned your back on this
new God," Drupadi murmured, keeping his voice low
enough so only the ears it was intended for could hear.

Patel eyed him silently.

"It is good you came to your senses, Patel," he continued. "My father told us of the concern of the council and
how they felt they must punish you if you did not return to
the old ways."

It was then that he saw the livid bruise on the other boy's
face, raised up like a small stone under the skin of his
cheekbone and already turned black. There was another on
his chin, and Drupadi wondered how bruised and cut his
back and shoulders were under his shirt.

There was no laughter in Patel's eyes, and at first Drupadi thought it must be because of the pain he was suffer-
ing. But when he spoke, Drupadi learned the truth.

"There is only shame in my heart this day," he murmured. "I know what my new God teaches. And I know in
my own heart what I believe. But when my father came to
me with fire in his eyes and a club in his hand I—I was
afraid!"

The other boy stared, disbelieving.

"I told my father I would turn my back on this new God
and come back to the old ways, but that was only to stop
the beating."

"Then—then you haven't given up the Jesus-way?" Drupadi could scarcely believe he was hearing his friend correctly.

Patel shook his head miserably. "This Jesus washed the sin from my heart and made me so I can go to heaven, and what do I do for Him?" Tears glistened in his solemn black eyes. "The first time I am asked, I say that I am turning my back on Him and am no more walking with Him!" The other boy's lips trembled. "What must He think of me?"

"But you can worship in secret," Drupadi told him. "No one can read what is in your heart."

Patel fought for control. "But don't you see? *He died for me!*"

It was all Drupadi could do to keep from crying himself. He turned away, fighting against it.

He was still standing there when one of the men of the village came running up.

"Where is Nala?" he cried. "Where is your father?"

Patel jumped to his feet.

"Your brother Ardjuna has been mauled by a tiger!"

4

Patel Hides

FEAR CAUGHT DRUPADI by the throat and shook him fiercely. The hated tiger had struck Patel's younger brother. It was, indeed, an act of vengeance set into motion by the gods. A great trembling took hold of him.

Patel sprinted off in the direction the villager pointed and Drupadi ran after him, unable to keep up with the flying feet of his friend. By the time they reached the place where Ardjuna was lying, blood oozing from a dozen knifelike slashes on his back, a crowd had gathered. Nala, his father, was bending over him and Sati, his mother, cradled his bloody head in her arms.

Patel stared down at them.

"He lives?" he asked, trembling.

No answer.

Drupadi saw that the injured boy was still alive. He stirred slightly and groaned.

"Patel angered the spirits," someone behind them muttered darkly. "Now Ardjuna suffers for it."

"He brings shame and vengeance to our village," someone else put in.

But the boy they were saying had caused the terrible trouble seemed not to hear their muffled voices.

"Does he live, my father?" he asked again.

Blazing eyes came up to meet his. "If he lives," Nala grated, "it is not because of you, my son."

A murmured chorus of agreement rippled over the crowd.

Drupadi watched as the men tenderly picked up Ardjuna and carried him back to the village. In spite of the fact that Patel was his closest friend, Drupadi felt himself being swept along by the thinking of the people. The coming of the tiger to their village after so long a time could not have been an accident. There was purpose behind it—a purpose everyone in Magadi knew. He thought of Ardjuna's still form and his handsome young face so twisted with pain.

Anger surged within Drupadi. This terrible thing that had happened to Ardjuna was Patel's doing. Even he had to admit it now. Why had his friend listened to the strange teacher when doing so was terrible enough to bring the wrath of the gods upon Magadi and was enough to turn everyone against him?

Word of the tiger's attack on Nala's younger son raced across the village. Women scooted their children into their huts with shrill, frightened cries to come inside and stay lest the *shere* get them. The men and older boys gathered grimly in the square. Most of the older ones had been on such expeditions before and dreaded what they had to do.

Sacuni led the hunting party down to the stream where Ardjuna had been attacked. Then they followed the stream first in one direction and then the other.

Drupadi was too young to go along. This was a job for the men and older boys whose arms were strong and their aim with the spear was good. He watched them leave, wanting to be one of them—to be in on the excitement and, above that, to be counted among the men. Yet, in a way, he was glad that he could stay behind. He could still feel how the terror crawled up his spine when he first saw the tiger's pug marks in the sand. It would be the same out on the hunt, he reasoned, even though there would be others at either elbow. It was good not to have to be out there.

A taut, apprehensive hush spread along the empty paths and enveloped the village. The children in their huts were affected by it so much that they talked in low tones, if at all. The women huddled inside, fearing for their husbands and their older sons.

Later, when the sun would hang on the rim of the mountain ridge before plunging the steep slope into darkness, there would be trips to the stream for water. The women would go hurriedly in a group, eyes constantly searching the bush around them with something akin to terror. After they returned the paths would be empty and desolate again.

Even Drupadi stayed inside, trying to quiet his uneasiness over Patel and the restless questioning of his mind.

Darkness came and the hunters still did not return. That could only mean that they had not yet found the *shere* and were still probing the countryside, trying to accomplish at night what they could not do in the light of day.

"It is time we go to bed, my son," Drupadi's mother told him.

Dutifully he helped her roll out the mats, trying not to think about his father and Kittu, or wondering where they were.

It was far into the night when they came stumbling home, exhausted.

Drupadi, who had been lying silently on his mat, unable to sleep for concern, rose on one elbow as Kittu came in.

"Did they find him, my brother?" he asked softly.

"The spirits are protecting the tiger well." He lay down on the floor beside his younger brother. "They are angered because of Patel and will not be denied their vengeance." He was parroting what he had heard the men on the hunt express.

Drupadi did not speak. He, too, felt that his friend was the source of the trouble with the tiger. He could not help it.

"Nala says that Patel took it back," the older boy whispered. "He said that he told him he was sorry for turning away from the gods of our people and that he was coming back and would no longer walk the way of this new God. But the elders want to hear it from Patel's lips. They want to be sure that he is telling Nala the truth."

Drupadi gasped audibly.

"What is it, my brother?" Kittu's sharp ears caught his surprise. "Do you fear for your friend if he goes before the elders?"

Drupadi snorted. "Why should I care if he goes before them? Why should it matter to me if they question him?"

"You should be glad for it," his older brother told him. "The *shere* threatens all of us."

Drupadi nodded. This he knew. But there were those gentle words of the white teacher to haunt him. He could only partially understand them, but they kindled a great longing in his heart. And, of course, Patel was his friend.

"Even now Nala and Sati have gone to the Temple of Rocks to offer sacrifices and pray for Ardjuna to get well," Kittu continued. "When they get back the council is going to call Patel before them to hear from his own mouth whether he turns back to our gods or no." His voice quavered. "It is the only way to rid our village of the curse of this bloodthirsty tiger."

There was a long, bleak silence.

"I am glad for you, my brother, that you were not with Patel that day," his older brother went on. "The people are angered. And the elders say that if Patel's father does nothing to punish him for what he has done, they will do it themselves. They fear that the gods might destroy the whole village if they don't."

Drupadi shuddered convulsively. It was even worse than he had supposed. He lay back on his pad and closed his eyes. But how could he sleep when his very soul was burning?

For the moment he forgot the tiger and the threat the beast was to the village. He could not let the villagers take his friend, at least without warning him. In their fear there was no way of knowing what they would do to him. There was no knowing what they would do to Drupadi either, if they caught him.

For a brief space of time he lay motionless, battling the matter in his mind. Then, cautiously, he turned over on his side and raised himself on one elbow. Kittu was the one he had to concern himself about. It would be difficult to slip out of the hut without waking his brother. But he thought he knew Kittu well enough to know that he wouldn't give him away if he did learn what he was about.

With caution Drupadi stood erect, inching stealthily around the sleeping form beside him. Kittu, exhausted from the long hunt and sleeping more soundly than usual, did not move. The slight, dark-skinned boy ducked out of the entrance into the black of the night.

The *shere!* He had not thought of him before. The tiger would be walking at night, as silently as a bird flying overhead or a sacred cobra slithering across the hard ground. He could creep up and pounce on him before Drupadi even knew the dread creature was near.

A spasm shook him violently. But he pushed forward, ignoring it. He had to talk to Patel—to warn him of what they planned to do.

Although the night was an opaque curtain even Drupadi's sharp eyes could not see through, he was so accustomed to the village paths that he moved without hesitation to the hut where Patel lived.

"Psssst!" he hissed, stealing close to the open entrance.

Instantly Patel spoke, as guardedly as he.

"Who is it?"

"It is I. Drupadi!"

His friend crept to the doorway.

"It's still the middle of the night," he whispered. "What are you doing here?"

"I've got to talk to you. The elders are angry, Patel," he said. "And Sacuni says he is going to call you before them once more as soon as your father returns from the Temple of Rocks."

"But why?" he demanded fearfully.

"They say the tiger was sent by the gods to bring vengeance on the village because of you. They want to question you themselves to be *sure* that you have turned your back on this new God, Patel."

Panic jerked the other boy's lithe body and glittered beneath dark eyelashes. His thin hand whipped out and grasped Drupadi's wrist.

"You speak the truth?"

Their eyes met.

"Would I lie to you of such a thing, my friend?"

Patel could feel the blood leave his gaunt face and the life seemed to go out of him. He brought his hand to the side of his face uneasily. He looked at Drupadi as though he was about to speak. but his lips parted wordlessly. He

was frightened in a way Drupadi had never seen before. It was a fright that reached down to the very roots of his soul for its beginning and surged up in great, pulsing waves that shook him violently.

"How do you know this to be?" Patel asked when he could force the words past his lips.

"Kittu told me. The men talked about it as they were on the tiger hunt."

Patel expelled his breath with a rush.

"Kittu said it was good that I was not with you," Drupadi continued, "or I would have been called before them too." The instant he started to give that information he was sorry for it, but it was too late.

Briefly hope gleamed in Patel's eyes.

"They would have called you before the council too?" he echoed, as though this was good news. "They must have some reason for that. Tell me, Drupadi, are you also a follower of Jesus?"

Drupadi recoiled involuntarily, slapped in the face by his friend's desperate question.

"Me?" He spit out the word as though it was bitter to the tongue. "Not me! I will never go against the ways of our fathers." His expression changed. He had not come to argue with his friend, he had come to inform him of what had taken place and what was going to happen next. He had come to plead with him to turn his back on this new God he was now following. "It was only because Kittu was fearful that I might walk the Jesus-way, since you are my friend, that he talked with me. He wanted me to know what will happen to you for your foolishness, and what would happen to me as well."

Patel glanced about uneasily. Drupadi knew he was

thinking about the beating his father had given him and was wondering what the council would do.

"The elders have no wish to be harsh," Drupadi continued. "They only want to please the gods so our village will be rid of the tiger and you will be worshiping again at the Temple of Rocks with your parents." A faint smile tugged hopefully at one corner of his mouth. "All you have to do is to tell them that you are going to come back to our ways!"

Despair rested briefly on Patel's tense face. "But I cannot!" His voice broke. "And with God's help, this time I will not!"

"Then you must leave!" Drupadi urged in hoarse tones. "You must leave now! While it is yet dark!"

Patel stared vacantly at him, as though the sudden happening had robbed his mind of reason. "But where can I go?" he asked helplessly. "Where can I go so they will not find me?"

Drupadi's active mind considered a dozen places. The thick bush along the stream would be good for hiding. And he and Patel had found many good spots far back in the forest where only the monkeys could find them. The monkeys and—Drupadi's blood chilled. The monkeys and the vicious, man-killing tiger who would probably be happier at killing Patel than a dozen other villagers.

Or his friend could go to the craggy spine of the mountain. The top of their great hill was a wild, rocky ridge with a road over the only pass most people knew about. Kittu had found another, a knife-crack between the sheer rock ledges, that led to the very top and over the other side. Kittu had taken Drupadi there once and had shown him the narrow slit that led to the opposite side.

"Nobody comes this way because of the sacred cobras," he said. "They love these rocks."

But that would not do for Patel. The sacred snakes would be as eager for his blood as the *shere* and the villagers. No, it had to be somewhere else.

"The cave!" he exclaimed aloud.

Patel's eyes gleamed. "No one would find me there!"

Drupadi didn't know why he hadn't thought of the cave at first. He and Patel had found it one day when they were herding their fathers' goats. And, as far as either of them knew, no one else had ever been to it.

It had been hot that afternoon and they were looking for a place out of the sun when they found the narrow crack in the side of the mountain, scarcely big enough for a person to squeeze through.

They had entered it fearfully the first time, sliding their feet cautiously over the hard clay floor and half expecting to find a cobra with each hesitant step. The next time they had gone to the cave, they had taken torches and explored it to the end. It was not a long cave, nor particularly wide. A man of average height could have stood up in it, but that was all. One as tall as Sahib Conway would have to duck or risk a bump on his skull. The cave was not particularly cool and there was no evidence that the sacred cobras they both feared and worshiped ever used it.

"Perhaps the cobras have been kind enough to leave it for us," Drupadi had observed.

Patel, however, had been thinking of something else. Even then it seemed that he did not have the proper respect for holy things.

"If we tell Kittu and the others about our cave they will not let us in."

Drupadi's eyes had sparked. "They won't find out about it!" he had affirmed. "We will tell no one!"

And so it had been. No one had been told about the cave. The boys had not even revealed their secret when their fathers saw the goats unattended, while they crouched inside. Their lips had remained silent later, although both had been beaten for leaving their flocks when they were supposed to stay with them.

Patel smiled his relief. "I'll go to the cave until this tiger is killed and the people forget about him and the shame and trouble I am supposed to have brought to Magadi."

"No one will find you there."

Patel hesitated. "But what of food?" he whispered. "And water? How will I live?"

"I will bring them!" his friend exclaimed loyally. Drupadi had not meant to make such a promise. After all, he was already suspected of going the Jesus-way, at least by Kittu. If he was caught helping his friend he would never be able to convince the council that he was not a believer the same as Patel.

And, worse, the tiger was still prowling the mountain slope seeking out victims!

But he had spoken. And when a person has spoken, that thing he must do, if he is going to be honorable and keep his word.

"You will come with food?" Patel asked, as though this was something he found difficult to believe.

"I will come with food and water. I promise." How could he do differently? How could he allow the villagers to take his friend when there was no knowing what terrible things they might do to him?

Patel's smile flashed. Then he spun on his heel and started away. But turning back impetuously, he took Drupadi by the hand in the manner of the white teacher. He shook it vigorously.

"You are my friend!"

With that he was gone, disappearing into the blackness of the night.

Relief surged over Drupadi. Patel was gone now. The villagers would never be able to find him! As he stood there, however, a vast uneasiness took hold of him. Going to the cave with food would be a greater risk than he had ever taken before. He would have to steal the food he took to Patel. Even his mother, who was gentle and soft of heart, would not give him food for Patel. He would have to sneak out of Magadi every day or so and make his way to the cave without being seen.

That was not going to be easy either. Even if no one else noticed, Kittu would. And it was likely that he would suspect where Drupadi was going. It was not a simple promise he had made to Patel.

But he pushed it forcibly to the outer rim of his consciousness. It did not have to be faced that day, at least. There would be time enough to be concerned on the morrow.

Slowly he began to move back to the hut where his family was sleeping. What was there about this God the teacher told about that would make Patel go off to a cave in the night, risking his life rather than come back to the gods of their fathers? It was more than Drupadi could understand.

5

Search Begins

As soon as dawn pushed the darkness away, the council came to Nala's hut for Patel. They had suspected that he might find out their plans for bringing him before them, and would escape unless they held him forcibly. They were prepared to do so, but he was not there.

"He is gone, Mukerji," they came to tell Drupadi's father while the boy trembled at the purpose of their visit. "He has escaped. Now the gods will be more angry than ever."

Mukerji gazed sagely at Sacuni. He was a wise man whose judgment was trusted. "Perhaps, my friend," he said quietly. "Perhaps not. The boy has gone out on the mountain, is it not so?"

"It is so."

"And where is the tiger?"

Slowly understanding spread across the elder's narrow, hollowed face.

"What better way of appeasing the gods is there than by letting the one who caused their anger become the victim of the *shere* they sent?" Mukerji continued.

Admiration warmed Sacuni's tired eyes. "It is good we have a wise man such as you in our village, Mukerji. You are a wise and holy man."

Drupadi looked away to keep them from reading the

52

horror that surged within him. What terrible thing was going to happen to his friend now?

Word that Patel had fled was noised quickly about the village. Some of the younger men, impetuous and strong-minded, rushed out to hunt for him in spite of the counsel of Sacuni and Mukerji. Later the other men in the village went out to look for the tiger. But neither group ranged far from Magadi or stayed long. Before dark both were back, empty-handed.

The next day Sacuni's judgment prevailed and both hunts were called off. "The one who caused our trouble and the one sent to avenge the gods are out there," he informed the men. "Let the *shere* have time to work his own revenge. If we interfere and kill the tiger before he has done his work, who knows? Something worse might befall us!"

Drupadi stood on the rim of the ragged group of men and listened, his own misery churning until he could scarcely think. How could he and Patel reason they could out-smart the gods? Didn't they know they were standing against the powers of the spirits? Even now the man-eater had probably sought out Patel and destroyed him for the terrible thing he had done.

And he was going to have to leave the village himself before long and make his way up to the cave. The tiger just might be waiting for him too. He trembled violently, and for a time he felt that he could not go. But he had to! Patel was his friend and he had given his word. There was nothing else for him to do.

He stole into the hut while his mother was at the market-place and got something for Patel to eat. He worked hur-riedly, listening for one of his younger brothers or sisters who had the embarrassing habit of popping in at the worst moment, bubbling with questions and babbling everything they learned as soon as one of their parents returned. Let one of them see what he was doing and he would be in fierce trouble.

Drupadi would have liked to take enough rice for two or three meals and be done with it, but that would never do, he told himself. His mother would miss the rice if so much were taken at one time. He would have to ration the food carefully. It would be better for him to take a little rice, some fish and a few pieces of fruit, because a little of each, stolen a small quantity at a time, would not be so likely to be noticed. Hurriedly he wrapped the food in a piece of cloth and stuffed it in the container he planned to take along for water.

Relief brought a smile to his lip. At least the first problem had been solved. He had enough for Patel to eat for a day or two and he had not been seen. Now to sneak out of the village and up to the cave! Perhaps this wasn't going to be so difficult, after all.

Determination in every movement, he ducked through the entrance into the blazing sunlight.

Kittu was standing nearby, suspicion narrowing his piercing black eyes. "You have food, my brother!" It was a declaration—a statement of fact.

It would not do for Drupadi to deny it. That would only make it worse. "What if I have?"

"Do you go to take food to that friend of yours?" his older brother asked, sneering. "The one who is going to be killed by the tiger?"

Drupadi's darkening gaze flamed angrily. "You know Patel, too! Have you taken food to him?"

"He is your friend, my brother!" Kittu snarled. "Not mine!"

"He is my friend, it is true." Drupadi's pulse beat furiously in the hollow of his throat, but his voice was firm and controlled. It had to be! One slip with Kittu and all would be lost. "But I am not so foolish as to risk the anger of the gods by taking food to him."

Drupadi flinched. What was he saying? Would the gods add his lying to the sin of helping Patel? Would even this add more to his punishment?

His older brother turned, a wavering smile folding the corners of his mouth upward. "Then you must be going to the Temple of Rocks to offer a sacrifice so Ardjuna will be spared and Patel will turn back to our ways and not suffer the anger of the gods."

"What if I am?" he demanded irritably.

Let Kittu think he was going up the mountain to the temple if he wanted to. It would make it easier for Drupadi to get food from home and would help to explain his absence from the village. It would help in another way, as well. Now Kittu half suspected that he was beginning to believe the white teacher and was in some way involved in Patel's disappearance from the village. There was no knowing when he could convince their father.

But if they thought he was sacrificing and praying at the temple, it would convince them all that he was not being influenced by either Patel or Sahib Conway. It could make things easier for him.

"You should hurry, Drupadi," Kittu said with unfamiliar concern. "You have far to go and it may be dark before you get back."

Drupadi planned on sneaking out of the village as inconspicuously as possible, depending on stealth to conceal his actions. But Kittu had unknowingly suggested another course of action by his assumption that Drupadi was going to the temple. It was better to go brazenly, as though he was

on an errand which he was making no attempt to keep
secret. To be furtive now would only cause suspicion.

Villagers nodded approvingly as they saw him walk past
their huts on his way out of the village and up the narrow,
dusty road in the direction of the Temple of Rocks.

"He is going up to pray," he heard a gray-haired man tell
his wife. "Mukerji has a dutiful son."

It was some distance out of the way for Drupadi to go in
the direction of the temple, but the extra walking meant
nothing to him. It was going to help him to deceive his
family and the rest of the villagers. That meant far more
than a few minutes' time.

When Drupadi was a mile or more from the village he
glanced over his shoulder to be sure he was not being
followed. Then he ducked off the road. The sun was still far
from setting; but now that it had begun to slip behind the
mountains, an opaque grayness seemed to spread across the
steep slope. Night was still some distance away, but the
darkness would creep up stealthily, providing a curtain to
shroud the movements of the tiger if he was about.

If what his father and Sacuni and the others said was
true, the tiger would be as interested in punishing him as
Patel. He was the one who had warned the other boy. He
had told him where to go, and now he was taking food to
him. Perhaps the *shere* was waiting, directed by Narada, the
messenger of spirits, until he approached.

His gaze darted furtively to one side and then the other,
sweeping each boulder, each scraggly clump of trees. There
were hiding places for the tiger everywhere he looked. His
fear pulsated in his temples and stole the red from his lips,
leaving them blue and trembling. He fought to control
himself and keep moving toward the cave when every fiber
of his being screamed for him to whirl and flee.

But he had given his word. He had to go on, step by step by step. It was the only way.

At last Drupadi reached the cave and his friend came out eagerly.

"I was afraid you were not going to come."

Drupadi's gaze met his evenly. One thing his father had taught him was to keep his word. "I told you I would come," he said simply, as though that was explanation enough.

Patel nodded. "I know." But his expression revealed that he had doubted him in spite of that. "I—I thought maybe you would be afraid."

"Me, afraid?" Drupadi retorted scornfully. He took the food out of the piece of cloth. "What makes you think I would be afraid?"

Patel hesitated. "Did they catch the *shere* yet?"

Drupadi knew why his friend was asking about the tiger. He was wondering if the dreaded beast might be coming up the mountain instead of staying along the stream. He was wondering if the tiger might find his way to the cave where he was hiding.

"Not yet," he answered. "They did not look for him today."

Patel caught the strange expression in his friend's voice. "Why did they stop hunting for the tiger?" he asked. "Was it because they were afraid?"

They were afraid, it was true. No one in his right mind would be unafraid of the tiger.

"That is not why they stopped," he informed Patel. "They want the *shere* to have time to take its revenge on you."

Patel's body jerked spasmodically, and it was a moment before he could speak. When he did, he changed the subject. "Only after I got here to the cave did I begin to think about how much you did for me, Drupadi. If it had not been for you—"

Drupadi's voice was harsh. "Why don't you come back, Patel?" he pleaded. "Come back and tell them you have changed your heart back to our gods. That is all they ask. They do not want the tiger to kill you; they do not want to hurt you. It is only to bring you back to the ways of our people that they do these things!"

Patel hesitated. Drupadi thought of the prayers for his friend that he would have said in the Temple of Rocks if he had gone there. Surely the gods would work in the heart of his friend and bring him to his senses!

"Please, my friend," Patel said. "It has been decided. I do not have the courage to go back and stand before the council and tell them I walk with this Jesus. And I cannot again say I no longer believe in Him. I can only stay here and hide, and pray that God will keep them from finding me."

Drupadi knew that it was useless to try to convince Patel against his will. He had set his heart and his mind in the Jesus-way. There was no changing him.

Drupadi said good-bye and left the cave, sprinting fearfully in the direction of the road. He was sure that every step would bring the ominous snarl of the tiger, its roar of rage and the knifelike slashing of its ugly claws into his back. But, though he ran until his lungs were bursting, there was no sign of the evil beast.

The hush of night was stealing in by the time he reached the village. Shadows blurred into shadows, marring the sharp, even lines of the huts and blotting out the desolate countryside. The paths were deserted and most of the huts were dark as Drupadi hurried into the village. His mother and father were waiting for him.

"I'm so glad you got back safely, my son," she murmured. "I feared the *shere—*" She could say no more.

"I told you, Khati, that the tiger would not harm our son," Mukerji reminded her. "You know where he went. The gods would not allow the tiger to harm him on his way back from the temple. We had nothing to fear."

He turned his attention to Drupadi. "Kittu told me where you went this afternoon," he said, approval warming his voice. "You are the sort of son who brings a glad heart to his father."

Drupadi squirmed uncomfortably. What if his father learned the truth? But his uneasiness soon gave way to relief. His father thought he had gone to the Temple of Rocks. That was better than he could have hoped for. He would have no difficulty now in getting away from the village, or even in getting food, so long as Mukerji thought it was going for sacrifices.

Every afternoon he wrapped some food in a piece of cloth and left the house boldly. Every day his father would ask about him and beam when his mother told him where he had gone.

"This, my son, brings honor to me, Khati," he would say. "When he was on earth before, he must have been a priest or a holy man."

Even Kittu was different toward Drupadi those days. No longer did he doubt and question every move. No longer was he suspicious of Drupadi and afraid that he would turn to the teacher's God. There was a friendliness and a concern in his attitude toward him that Drupadi had not seen before.

With the passing of each day Patel's melancholy seemed

to grow. He was lonely in the cave and tried to keep Drupadi there with him on one pretext or another as long as he could. And he was concerned about how long he would have to hide there.

"Is it all right if I come home now?" he would ask when Drupadi came with something for him to eat.

"Not yet. The talk is still bad against you."

There was a desperate pleading in his eyes. "When do you think I can go back home, my friend?" he asked.

Drupadi wanted to tell him that it would be all right for him to go back when he was ready to tell the council that he was turning his back on his new God and was no longer going to walk the Jesus-way. But he knew that would not do any good. There was nothing in Patel's manner that indicated he was ready to confess the new way was wrong.

"The tiger attacked a herd of goats yesterday and killed two before he was driven away," Drupadi said. "Now the people are upset again. It is not good for you to come back to our village yet."

But even that did not cause Patel to weaken, or so it seemed to Drupadi.

6

Suspicion Grows

THE NEXT TIME the teacher and his son came to the village the sahib had his rifle along.

"If some of your men will go out and help me," he told Sacuni, "I will try to kill this tiger for you."

A ripple of approval ran through the elders who made up the council. Mukerji's admonition to give the tiger time to track down Patel and take vengeance for the gods was all but forgotten as the men looked upon the rifle.

Drupadi knew what they were thinking.

There was the sort of weapon to use on a *shere*. It was one thing to go out after him with spears and sticks, knowing they had to move in close enough to use such feeble tools against the power in those dreadful claws and those great, tearing teeth. It was quite another to have a rifle along that could spit death half across the mountain. Any man could be brave with such a force of destruction in his hands.

Drupadi stole close enough to admire the powerful rifle. For a moment or two he let his gaze run along the dark barrel and study the beautiful wood in the stock. Such a weapon did not look dangerous at all, but he had heard such a rifle roar once two or three years before, and had seen the tree that it had almost torn in two. With a gun like that, surely Sahib Conway could kill the tiger and remove the curse from their distraught village.

"It is not good to go after the tiger with sticks and spears," one of the elders said, giving voice to the thoughts of all of them.

Only Mukerji opposed the hunt, but he did not voice his protest. Drupadi read his father's opposition in his black eyes and, trembling, moved back into the crowd, hoping Mukerji had not seen him.

As soon as the people learned the teacher was going after the tiger with a rifle, the men and boys flocked to help. They brought their spears and clubs and laughingly took their places in the hunting party. It was different shouldering such a weapon when they knew there was going to be a rifle along.

While the crowd was getting organized to leave Magadi, Jack came over to the place where Drupadi was standing. "I was looking for you when we came in, but I didn't see you," he said.

Drupadi did not answer. How could he explain to his friend that he had been hiding in the crowd so his own father would not see him?

"Are you going along to hunt the tiger?" he asked.

"I wouldn't miss it."

Drupadi examined the white boy's youthful face wistfully. He, too, would like to go along on the hunt. It might give him a chance to slip away from the hunting party once they were on the mountain and get some more food to Patel. But, more than that, he would like to be along to see the sahib use the rifle. He would like to see the tiger destroyed, to be there when this threat to Magadi was removed. But he was too shy and too polite to ask.

"Would you like to go with us?" Jack inquired.

Would he! His eyes brightened.

"I'll meet you down by the stream," he whispered cautiously, "where we first saw the pug marks. They will go that way."

Jack eyed him curiously. Drupadi knew he was wondering why he didn't go along now and why he wanted to meet the hunting party away from the village. But he asked no questions.

Drupadi sneaked out of the village even before the hunting party left, and made his way down to the mountain stream to wait for them. He was quite sure that his father had not seen him, but that was a risk he would have to take. Such an event as this would be well worth the beating he would probably get.

But he need not have been so careful, he saw quickly. Kittu was with the men and waved to him. His father would have wanted his sons to help with the hunt, he realized. Their family should have a share in the glory if that dread beast was to be destroyed that day. He was only doing what his father would have wanted him to do.

The hunting party went to the place where the tiger had attacked the flock of goats and fanned out on either side of Sahib Conway. The teacher was walking a pace or two ahead of the others, his rifle ready. Slowly they made their way through the thick growth along the stream.

Drupadi felt the perspiration moisten his arms, and his skin crawled with excitement. In spite of the rifle and his closeness to the teacher, dry, coppery fear tasted bitter in his mouth. It was a fearsome thing to move through the bush when he knew there was a tiger somewhere near. With every step he peered intently into the tangle of trees and brush ahead, expecting to see the ugly beast crouching there, waiting for them to draw close enough to pounce on them.

He could not help thinking of what his father had said. The tiger could not be killed by spears or the bullets of men until he accomplished what the gods had sent him to do. Looking at the rifle in the village, Drupadi had been certain it would stop any tiger. Now, in the forest, he was not so sure.

He felt the food he had secreted under his shirt—the food he hoped to slip to Patel if he could get away from the others long enough. But, perhaps the gods would tell the *shere* of his plans so he could lie in wait for him near Patel's hiding place. Perhaps this was an evil trick by the gods to punish him for giving help to his friend.

The thought brought such consternation to Drupadi's

face that Jack, looking at him, thought he must be ill.

"What's the matter? Don't you feel good?"

The Indian boy glanced his way, black eyes narrowing. "I feel all right. Why?"

"You sure don't look it."

"It—it is the tiger," Drupadi said. "I am afraid we will not get him today."

"Then we will try again," his white companion said confidently.

At last they came to a place where the tiger had made a kill, a small animal of some sort. But there was not enough of it left to even be able to tell what it was when one of the men held up a bit of hair and hide he found amid the blood on the ground.

"See!" he cried. "The tiger was here last night!"

For a time they stood in an excited knot, talking about it rapidly. It was Sacuni who suggested building a platform in the trees and staking out a goat as bait.

"The *shere* may come back here," he said.

"That sounds like an excellent idea," the teacher replied. "I'll help build the *machan* in the trees if you want to have some boys get a goat."

"Come on, Drupadi," Jack said quickly. "We'll get the goat. OK?"

The Indian boy was not sure that he wanted to help get the goat for such a trap. Sacuni had not asked him to, for one thing, and among their people it was always the leader who made such decisions. Everyone else waited for him to speak. For another thing, Drupadi wasn't sure he wanted to walk back to the village with only Jack to go with him. It was bad enough going up the mountain to the cave where his friend was hiding to take food to him. Here there was evidence that the tiger was close. He could be anywhere in the bush, watching them, following them. So Drupadi waited.

But in a moment the village leader nodded. "It is good, Drupadi," Sacuni said. "Go to your father and tell him we must have one small goat to bait the *machan*." He must have read the new concern that flashed in the boy's eyes. "Tell him I sent you."

Drupadi and Jack hurried away. At the same time others went back to Magadi for two *charpoys,* crude Indian beds which would be hoisted into the tree and tied there upside down to form a platform or *machan* for the hunters to sit on.

An hour before dark all was in readiness.

"Now," Sahib Conway said, "I will need some sharp eyes to watch for me."

Drupadi glanced hopefully at his friend. It would be too much to expect that he would be permitted to join them.

"You can come," Jack said. "I already talked to my father about it."

The teacher looked over the others, but before he could make a choice Sacuni spoke once more. "I will stay," he announced.

It was crowded with the four of them on the *machan,* but Jack was not large and neither was Drupadi or Sacuni.

"How long will we stay?" the Indian boy whispered.

"All night, maybe," the teacher replied. "You're going to be cold without a coat."

The boy shook his head. He would be cold, that was true. But he was used to being cold at night. He had no coat to bring even if he had known they were going to spend the night there. He had reached the place where he had learned to ignore the cold.

The men on the *machan* sat motionless, peering intently

into the trees that surrounded the small open place where the frightened little goat was tied, straining to catch a glimpse of that stealthy, tawny form they hoped would soon come inching out of the bush to get the goat.

Drupadi felt sorry for the terrified little animal that was bleating so plaintively. He would have liked to skin down the tree and turn the little animal loose. But even as the impulse swept over him, he knew it was wrong.

This was not a game so the sahib could say he had killed a tiger. It was deadly serious. If all went well the tiger would be killed before it got to the goat, but it was better that a goat should die than that the *shere* should claim the life of one of the villagers.

Silently the night closed in, stealing across the mountain on shadowy tiptoes to blot out the trees, blending them together in a seamless curtain that even the night-trained eyes of Sacuni and Drupadi could not see through.

The goat bleated even more pitiably, but that was the only sound. Grimly the hunters waited, not even talking in whispers. Sahib Conway held the rifle with both hands. Sacuni had the powerful flashlight he was to switch on if the tiger came for their bait.

The hours crept by, moving endlessly, with the same tireless deliberation of the length of the dry season, stretching from sun to sun to sun. Drupadi had almost fallen asleep, wrapped in the misery of the chill night air, when there was a faint rustling noise somewhere below them. He pulled himself erect quickly, listening. The sound came once more, not unlike the stealthy footsteps of a man.

He reached out silently and touched the hunter's arm with a trembling forefinger in warning. Conway's head turned to indicate that he got the message, but he did not speak.

Drupadi pointed in the direction from which the sound had come. By this time Sacuni was pointing the flashlight in that direction, waiting for Conway's signal to flip the switch and flood the area with the powerful beam of light.

The sound ceased momentarily and Drupadi's heart faltered. The tiger either had heard them or gotten their scent. He must know there was something that wasn't right about the goat being tied out in the bush alone.

They waited. Presently the sound came again. Sahib Conway motioned for Sacuni to switch on the light, but he hesitated for an instant. Then there was a thin, metallic snap and the beam of light stabbed a great, symmetrical hole in the darkness.

Drupadi's eyes picked out a faint tawny shape behind the leaves and twigs directly in the center of the beam of light. The teacher slammed the rifle to his shoulder and squinted through the telescopic sight. Drupadi braced himself for the sudden explosive blast of the gun, but it did not come.

"Shoot!" Sacuni whispered hoarsely.

But it was too late. The sudden blinding light had held the great cat paralyzed for a few precious seconds, but then it had leaped away to escape in the safety of darkness.

A full minute passed before anyone could speak.

"Didn't you see him?" Jack asked at last, his voice mirroring his disappointment.

"I saw him, but I only saw a patch of his body," the teacher explained, almost defensively it seemed to Drupadi. "I couldn't shoot without knowing for sure that I would hit a vital spot and kill him. A wounded tiger would be an even worse menace to the people than he is now."

"We will go home," Sacuni announced in poorly hidden disgust. "The tiger will not come back tonight."

They led the little goat back to the village in silence.

The next morning Mukerji got a complete report of what had happened on their nighttime hunt from his younger son.

"It is not good for one such as the sahib to be among us," he said when Drupadi had finished. "I opposed it from the beginning when he asked for permission to come here and teach. I oppose it now. No good can come to our village as long as he is allowed to twist the minds of our people."

"But, my father!" Drupadi exclaimed, reckless in his concern for his white friends. "Sahib Conway did not shoot because he was afraid of wounding the tiger and making him more of a danger than he is now. You know how bad a wounded tiger can be."

Mukerji did not even hear what he had said. Not really. He seemed to be much too concerned with his own thoughts.

"He did not shoot, my son," he intoned slowly, "because the spirits stopped him. They are determined to bring shame and harm to Magadi because of the teaching we permit here!"

Drupadi shuddered fearfully. He knew his father well. He was not simply talking about telling the teacher and his son that they could no longer come back to Magadi to teach. That would be a small matter, although he would not like to lose these new friends. Those dark flames in Mukerji's eyes spoke of something far more serious—something that his son could not fully understand, but could only guess at. And it troubled him.

7

Drupadi Tells

DRUPADI STIRRED RESTLESSLY and opened his eyes. Kittu was still breathing heavily on his mat beside him, his thin form covered by a ragged piece of cloth. Nothing marred Kittu's rest. He lay there peaceably, unmindful of the early morning cold or the turmoil that kept his younger brother from sleeping.

The early morning light was just beginning to show itself. Long gray spears edged silently over the mountain, pushing the night into doorways and driving it into hollows and corners and clumps of brush.

Drupadi sat up, shivering. His parents still slept, and so did his younger brothers and sisters, all lying on the hard-packed dirt floor of the one-room hut. They, too, were unaware that the night had been tortuous for him, and that the coming of daylight had done nothing to calm him. The throbbing uneasiness that kept him awake still lay unmelting within.

The white teacher and his son, Jack, had stayed in the village guesthouse that night. He saw Sacuni take them there when they got back from the tiger hunt. Drupadi fervently wished that they had gone back to their own village without even waiting to sleep.

To be sure, the only threats he had heard that were directed at them came from the lips of his own father. And it could be that they were not threats at all, but only the expression of bewilderment and fear. What Mukerji had said would have meant little except for the fact that he was an honored and respected man in the village and had been opposed to the sahib being allowed to teach in Magadi at all. Drupadi did not think his father would stir up the villagers against his friends. He was a just and honest man and wise in all his ways. But the night before, there had been fear gleaming darkly—fear that unless something was done, tragedy would befall their village. That could change his father into a man he did not know—a man who might be capable of anything.

Drupadi pushed aside the thin coverlet and was about to get to his feet when his father moved. Quickly he lay back down and closed his eyes. For a brief space of time he held his young body rigid, fear tightening its hold upon him like a python tightening its coils until he had to fight to breathe.

He didn't know what wild recklessness had come over him to cause him to try to leave the hut so early, and with the teacher still in the village. His father was sure to have missed him and linked his absence with the sahib and his son. The very thought was enough to leave Drupadi trembling.

Feigning sleep, he lay on his mat until the rest of the family was up. Only then did he dare to leave the house. He sauntered down the path in the opposite direction of the guesthouse, keeping a wary eye for Kittu or anyone else from the family. When he was sure he was safely out of sight he darted to one side and slithered back in a long, circuitous route that gave wide berth to his own hut. Cautiously he approached the guesthouse.

The teacher and his son were already up, and a small cluster of men and boys was gathered about them. Sacuni

was there, his gaunt, dusky face set as hard as stone against Sahib Conway.

"No!" The word was harsh. "We will not furnish beaters to help you."

"But we know where the tiger is now," the teacher protested. "If we have a little help I'm sure we can find and kill him."

The village leader was unmoved. "If any man in Magadi goes with you, he goes alone."

The teacher looked beyond Sacuni to the ragged semi-circle behind him. "How about it?" he asked. "How many of you will help me?"

No answers. Their faces were as hard and unfriendly as Sacuni's.

"But you were all anxious to go yesterday."

"That was yesterday," the elder reminded him darkly.

"But things haven't changed," Conway said, exasperated. "The *shere* is still as dangerous to you and your women and children as ever."

"We will not go with you, Sahib," Sacuni repeated. "You are powerless to kill the tiger. The gods will not allow you to shoot!"

Conway studied the sullen, frightened faces incredulously. Drupadi thought he might try to argue with them, but he realized that the teacher also read their resolve and knew it would be useless.

"If you won't go with me." he said. "I'll go alone."

Jack glanced at his youthful Indian friend. "Can Drupadi and I go with you?" he asked.

Drupadi inhaled sharply. His white friend had blurted the question for all to hear. Someone would surely catch the implication and tell his father. Then he would be in great trouble.

The sahib hesitated, eyeing Drupadi in silence. "I don't think it would be wise, Jack," he said. "You had better wait for me in the village. I won't be gone too long."

Drupadi pivoted and moved away with great reluctance. He was conscious of the fact that he had turned his back on his friend—conscious also that there were other eyes peering at him. His father was sure to find out from Sacuni or one of the others what had happened that morning, and he would question his son until he learned the truth.

He had hurried some distance along the path when he heard the sound of running feet behind him. Color crept up his neck and steel claws clutched relentlessly at his throat. He knew who was following him even before he heard Jack's voice.

"Hey, Drupadi! Wait for me!"

Uneasily he stopped and turned.

"Man, you took off in a rush," he said. "I was afraid I wasn't even going to get a chance to talk to you."

Drupadi coughed. "I—I—"

"What's wrong, Drupadi?" Jack insisted, his voice a whisper. "Why don't they want my father to kill the tiger?"

The Indian boy looked down without speaking.

"Are they afraid of something?"

"I don't know," Drupadi lied. "You will have to ask them." He could not tell his friend what was really wrong. He could not repeat to him what the people were saying. He started away.

"Where are you going?" Jack asked. "I thought we could go out and play ball or something."

Drupadi's anxious gaze drifted uneasily from one hut to the other. No one seemed to be watching them, or even noticing who he was talking with, but he could not be sure.

"I've got to do something first," he said lamely. "I'll meet you at the stream."

Jack's forehead crinkled seriously. "At the stream?" he echoed. "That's close to where we saw the tiger last night."

Drupadi started. He was in such turmoil that he had completely forgotten the tiger. "It is so," he whispered. "Let us meet on the road up the mountain, beyond the third turn."

That was far enough away to avoid being seen by the tattlers in the village.

"So far?" There was suspicion in Jack's voice.

Drupadi quickly replied, "I go now. I will see you there as soon as I have finished what I have to do."

His first thought had only been to get away from Jack before the situation got any worse than it was—before there was anything more for the people to tell his father. But, as he hurried away, he remembered that he had not taken Patel anything to eat the day before. There had been no chance for him to get away from the hunting party during the day, and when the teacher decided to make the platform in the tree and bait the trap with a goat, he had been so excited that he completely forgot his friend's food.

He went back to the hut, hoping as he did so that he would be able to get something for Patel without being caught at it. But Kittu was there again. His brother was always around when he didn't want him to be. Drupadi stormed inwardly. It was almost as though Kittu was hanging around, spying on him.

"What are you going to do when they decide to drive your friends away?" he taunted.

Drupadi's cheeks flamed, but he pushed past his brother and went inside. He was hoping Kittu would go somewhere else before he had to steal food again. He wasn't sure how many trips to the Temple of Rocks a suspicious one like Kittu would believe. But his older brother would not leave as long as he was home, it seemed. He followed him inside, watching him intently.

"Our father will learn that you went to the guesthouse this morning, Drupadi," he predicted. "He will learn that the younger one is friendly enough with you to ask the sahib if he can take you with them after the tiger."

Drupadi got some rice from the family stores. He wasn't able to get as much as he would have liked, but with Kittu there, he did not dare take more.

"Are you going to the temple again?" His doubt was evident in his voice.

Drupadi took a piece of fish and two small cakes to add to the rice he still had.

"What is it to you, my brother?"

Kittu leered at him. "It is strange that you have only now started going to the temple," he said. "Now that Patel is hiding somewhere out on the mountain." He gestured widely with his hand.

Drupadi kept his gaze lowered as he wrapped the food in a piece of cloth. What did Kittu know about him? Or did he know anything at all? Drupadi would have liked to question him, to have led him on until he found out for sure; but as it was he dared not say anymore than was necessary. He dared not allow his brother to see into his eyes, so fearful was he of what might be revealed there.

"You can go with me if you want to," he said bravely, not knowing what he would do if Kittu should decide to accept his invitation. Jack Conway would be waiting for him up the road they would have to take to get to the temple.

The older boy laughed. "I would rather follow you," he teased. "I would learn much more that way."

Drupadi shrugged in a vain attempt to hide his concern.

"You can follow if you want to, or you can go with me. Then you'll know I'm going to the Temple of Rocks."

Drupadi left the hut, his brother's laughter still quickening his pulse. He would have to be careful about pretending he was going to the temple to pray. Even Nala and Sati, who had gone there to pray for the healing of their son, had only made a few trips. If he persisted, someone was sure to suspect that he was going somewhere else. And if that word got to his father, he didn't know what would happen.

He made his way casually to the edge of the village, as though heading for the stream. Once he was beyond the narrow line of trees that would screen him from the village, he doubled back, circling Magadi, and trudged up the steep dirt road to the place where Jack was waiting.

"Hi." His friend grinned up at him from his place beneath a *niagroda* tree at the side of the rough road.

"Greetings."

"I was beginning to think that you weren't coming."

"I had more to do than I thought," he lied.

Jack scrambled to his feet. "Well, you're here. And I guess that's all that matters." He looked at the bundle under Drupadi's arm. "What'd you do, bring something to eat?"

"Yes—I mean—" The words caught. He *had* brought something to eat; he could not deny that. "Only it's not for me," he continued lamely.

Jack was curious but asked no questions. Drupadi weighed the situation. For some reason he hadn't even considered the fact that if he went up to the cave that morning he would have to take Jack into his confidence. Now he had no choice except to tell his friend everything.

"And I am the only one who knows where Patel is," he concluded in a tense whisper.

Jack was incredulous. "You mean this happened because Patel decided to follow the true God?"

Drupadi nodded. "And because the *shere* came," he added, "the people say he was sent by the gods to punish our village. It happened because Patel forsook the ways of our people."

Fear burned in Jack's eyes. "That's terrible. What will they do if they find him?"

Drupadi shuddered. "Who can tell what they might do to Patel if they find him? They might beat him and let him go. They might stone him. There are many ways of punishment."

"Will he ever be able to come back to the village if they don't catch him?" Jack continued.

"That is something else that no one knows. They might remember the terrible thing he did in spite of the many days that have passed. Or they might forget, as though it had never happened. But Patel cannot depend on that."

"Where is Patel now?"

"Out there." He gestured widely. "In a secret cave we found."

"You take the food up to him while I go back to the village. My father will be in early this afternoon. I'll go back and talk to him; he might be able to help."

Drupadi didn't know what they might be able to do for his friend, but he was glad to be able to talk with someone about him. He didn't feel so helpless and alone anymore.

8

Patel Is Found

Cautiously Drupadi made his way over the rough mountainside to the cave where Patel was hiding, bare feet ignoring the stone and stubble he had crossed. His friend came to meet him fearfully.

"You are late." Patel's voice addressed Drupadi, but even as he spoke his eyes searched the bleak slope. "Do they know where I am? Did they follow you?"

"Not yet, but Kittu has begun to wonder."

Patel's cheeks faded and fear glazed his eyes. He knew and feared Kittu even as Drupadi did.

"I have to go or he will find me! I won't stay here any longer!"

"That's one of the things I wanted to tell you. Maybe you won't have to stay here. Maybe you can cross the mountain with the teacher." Hurriedly he explained about confiding in Jack and that their white friend was going to talk to his father and get him to help.

"That is good." Patel sighed. "You tell him I'll go with him, Drupadi. I'll go quickly!"

Drupadi glanced up at the blazing sun. "I have to hurry now," he told Patel. "I'm to meet the sahib and Jack on the road."

He left the food with his friend and hurried off to meet the white teacher and his son once more. The jeep was pulled off to the side of the road and they were waiting for him when he got there.

Jack had told his father much of what had happened to Patel on their way from the village. All that remained for Drupadi was to answer the sahib's questions.

"I'm beginning to understand a lot of things," the white teacher said. "I see now that that's the reason no one would go with me and help track down the tiger."

"They were afraid," Drupadi told him. "They thought the gods were protecting the *shere* and would not let you shoot. They were afraid you could do nothing while the tiger tore them in pieces."

The tall white teacher's face lighted briefly. "That explains a lot of things." He paused. "And what of Patel?" he asked. "What will happen to him now?"

"I talked to him this morning," Drupadi answered. "He wants you to take him away so the elders of Magadi cannot hurt him."

Sahib Conway jerked erect. "He wants to leave home for good?" he echoed, as though he could not quite believe it. "Is it actually that serious?"

"They will do bad things to him."

"You're sure of that?"

Drupadi's chin bobbed in a quick nod. "They say it is the only way the gods will let them kill the tiger and spare Magadi."

The teacher's eyes gleamed, and for the first time Drupadi saw fear glinting darkly in them. It was not true, he told himself. The sahib could not be afraid of the gods. There had to be some other reason for his concern.

"I wish there were something I could do," he said at last.

"You mean you can't help him?" his son demanded. "You can't help Patel?"

Drupadi's gaze fastened on the teacher's solemn face. He was so kind and good, he couldn't leave Patel without helping him now that he was in such deep trouble. After all, it had been the things he told Patel that had caused him to forsake the old ways and to run away. It was because Patel was following his teaching about this new God that he was hiding alone in the cave. It was the sahib's fault. He could not turn his back on Patel now. *He had to help!*

The white teacher spoke again. "I wish there were something I could do."

Drupadi did not give voice to the thoughts that tumbled wildly in his mind, but his eyes revealed his own bewilderment and a silent accusation that was just beginning to form.

"It's this way," the sahib tried to explain, desperation tightening his voice. "Nala and Sati are Patel's parents. He belongs to them and is supposed to do what they tell him until he is grown."

"But the villagers want to hurt him!" Drupadi cried. "They might even kill him!"

Still the teacher would not say that he would help Patel escape.

"They might claim that I stole Patel from them," he continued. "They might get the police and have me put in jail for it, or drive me out of the country and never let me come back."

The sahib made it sound as if it would be very bad if he helped Patel. Drupadi did not understand all of it, but he realized that it could be very bad for the teacher if he did help Patel to get away from his parents and the elders.

"But we've got to do something," Jack broke in. "We can't let them find him!"

Conway was silent for a time, thinking.

"Is it really as bad as that, Drupadi?" he persisted. "Is Patel's life actually in danger unless he is gotten out of reach of the people?"

It was hard for Drupadi to answer such a question. Who could know for sure what the elders would do when they found Patel?

"Maybe yes," he said. "Maybe no." There was great anger in the village over what had happened, he told the teacher. And the people were very afraid.

When he finished he looked up at the sahib breathlessly, trying to read his decision in his eyes.

"I think you fellows are right," he said at last. "We can't leave him where he is if they're going to do something bad to him. We'll have to get him to Chalama and off to a school or into some home where the villagers can't get at him!"

Relief flashed in Drupadi's eyes. He was so sure the sahib would do something to help—so sure that he would not leave Patel to hide until the villagers found him or until he was forced to come home. Now he knew that his friend was going to escape.

"We'll go up and get him," Jack's father said, starting the engine suddenly, "if you'll ride along to guide us."

"Sure! I'll go along!" Eagerly Drupadi clambered into the rear seat of the jeep and pointed out the rough, rocky trail to the cave.

He hadn't known he could feel so good. In a few minutes Patel would be out of the cave and on his way to the mountain pass and safety where he need not be afraid of

Sacuni or Mukerji or his father, Nala. And Drupadi would not have to risk being discovered taking food up to him.

It was only two or three miles over to the cave, but the climb was so steep the sturdy jeep was only able to creep along. The minutes passed slowly as they struggled upward in the dusty, shimmering heat of the afternoon. They were not far below the cave when Drupadi heard a sudden, triumphant shout above the tortured growling of the engine. Conway lurched to a stop.

"What was that?"

Drupadi pointed a wavering finger in the direction of the cave. They could not see the entrance, but they were near enough to see a handful of villagers.

"Look!"

While they stared the men from the village turned Patel around and shoved him along the trail ahead of them.

Drupadi's eyes widened. They were too late! The people had already captured Patel!

The villagers had been so excited at finding the boy who had been hiding from them that the presence of the jeep did not attract their attention until the teacher swung it around in a cramped turn and jammed the footfeed to the floorboards.

"Get down, Drupadi!" he cried in a hoarse whisper. "Get down!"

The vehicle lurched over the rough, stony mountainside, gathering speed as it went. Drupadi crouched on the floor, clinging desperately to the seat. They didn't see him, he reasoned in desperation. They couldn't have! He had been the first to spy them and had scooted out of sight even before the teacher told him to. He didn't have to be afraid that he had been seen!

But his relief died as quickly as it came with a quick spasm that almost stopped his heart from beating. Kittu had looked strangely at him in the hut that morning. And he had spoken with disquieting sarcasm, as though he knew far more than he was saying. Perhaps the elders of Magadi had already known that he was helping Patel and had only been waiting for the right opportunity to capture him.

If that was true, his trouble was as great as Patel's! His slender body jerked. He could not even imagine what terrible thing his father might do to him for such disobedience and for helping one who was out of favor with the gods. Such turmoil churned within him that he could not think; he could not breathe.

Not until they reached the road did the sahib slow the wildly lurching vehicle. Then he jammed on the brakes and screeched to a halt in a billowing curtain of dust.

"We'd better let you out here, Drupadi," he said, looking

hurriedly about to see if they were being watched by anyone. "It wouldn't do for us to be seen taking you into the
village now that they know we were on our way up to see
Patel."

"Oh, no!" Drupadi retorted quickly, vaulting from the
rear seat of the jeep. Whatever happened, he could not be
seen with the teacher and his son now. That would only
make things worse than they were already. "It is much
better that I walk."

"We'll be back in a week, Drupadi," the sahib assured
him. "And we'll be praying for both Patel and you."

The boy scarcely heard him. He spun on one bare foot
and sped down the hot, dusty road. He had to get back
before the villagers returned with Patel. He had to be able
to pretend that he had been in Magadi all the time. Even
that would not be successful if someone had recognized him
in the sahib's jeep, or if Kittu had, indeed, followed him up
to Patel's hiding place. But it was the only thing he could
do. It was his only chance of escaping punishment.

What terrible thing would happen to his friend now that
they had caught him, Drupadi did not know. He dared not
even allow himself to think about it.

The villagers would haul Patel before the council first,
and Sacuni or one of the other elders would tell the charge
against him. Those who knew anything about it would be
asked to speak out. Someone would tell how he had said
boldly before them all that he was turning away from the
old gods in order to follow the new God the teacher talked
about. Others would explain about the tiger and how the
gods must have sent him to punish them for what the boy
had done.

All of these things everyone knew, but even a person like
Patel who had brought shame and trouble to the village was

entitled to have the council sit in judgment on what he had done. That was the law of their people. It would be different with the sahib and his son if action were taken against them. They were not of the village; they would not be judged according to their customs.

When everything had been presented against him, Patel would be given a chance to speak. Then, if he told them he was again turning back to their old gods and would no longer listen to the white teacher with his strange words, they would probably beat him and let him go.

But who could know what his friend would do? Bewilderment and fear mingled in Drupadi's dusky face. This God of the white teacher seemed to have some strange hold on Patel that caused him to feel shame because he had not told his father that the new God owned his heart when his father beat and questioned him. Perhaps this time he would act as foolishly as he had talked when Drupadi was with him. Then he would be in more trouble than he had ever known before.

Nearing the village, Drupadi slowed to a walk. He could not have people see him as he was now, lungs heaving from exertion and sweat soaking his shirt and ragged trousers. He had to stop his labored breathing and let the hot sun dry the sweat on his body if he was to convince the people that he had not left Magadi.

Drupadi glanced about, desperation glittering in his slitted eyes. Where would he tell them he had been, if they asked him? He could tell them he had been with some of his friends, he reasoned; but if the council doubted him, they could too easily prove he was deceiving them. It would be better to say that he had been along the stream looking for stones.

To be sure, he had been forbidden to go to the stream

alone until the tiger was destroyed. So he might get a beating from his father for disobeying, but it would be better than having everyone learn the truth.

He turned off the road and circled the village so he would be coming in on the other side, as he would if he had been to the stream.

The white teacher said this new God did not like it when a person lied. That was one of the things that caused Patel so much trouble as he considered how he had lied to his father about walking with the teacher's God. Lying had never bothered Drupadi before, but now the thought that he was preparing another lie to tell his own father and the people of the village squirmed uneasily into his consciousness.

Angrily Drupadi tried to push his uneasiness aside. He wasn't following the sahib's God, he reasoned. He was staying with the old ways of his people. And, as long as he didn't think about what the teacher said, it didn't bother him when he told things that were not true.

He entered the village cautiously with feigned carelessness. He wanted to be seen so there would be those to speak for him in case the council doubted his story. But he didn't want to be stopped by anyone because he was too choked up inside to try to talk.

There were those who spoke to him, but no one seemed to notice where he came from or to be curious about what he had been doing. He made his way to his father's hut and ducked inside. His mother looked up.

"Drupadi!" she exclaimed. "I am so glad you're back!"

He squinted narrowly at her. It was strange she would be so concerned about his being away for a while. He was often gone all day.

"Did you hear?" she continued. "They found Patel!"

His eyes dilated. The men weren't back yet. How could she know?

"W-was he hiding close by?" he asked, trying to sound surprised but not too concerned. "He wasn't hiding in the village, was he?"

"Kittu found him," she exclaimed, pride slipping into her voice. "He came back and got your father and Sacuni and the others."

Drupadi exhaled noisily, the color going out of his brown cheeks. It was Kittu, then. He must have followed him and Jack up the mountain and saw where Patel was hiding. Perhaps he had even followed him before and only now decided that he should tell the others. That must have been what his older brother had been hinting at when they talked that morning.

Drupadi writhed. That meant Kittu knew everything. He felt as though icy fingers throttled his windpipe.

As soon as the men got back to the village they would come for him. And whatever punishment Patel got, he would get as well. An almost uncontrollable fear engulfed him and for a brief, fluttering heartbeat all he could think about was to flee while there was still time for him to get away.

But he had to be careful or he would only make matters worse. Kittu was his brother and had listened to the teacher too. It could be that he had not told their father and Sacuni of Drupadi's part in Patel's escape from the village and hiding in the cave. It was already obvious that he had not told their mother.

It might be better to hide in the shadows and see what happened, Drupadi decided. If he watched closely, he should soon be able to tell if they were looking for him.

He was still standing in the entrance to their thatched hut

when there was a commotion at the far edge of the village
—a great shouting and yelling as the people surged in that
direction.

"They've come back, Drupadi!" His mother darted out of
the hut and, raising the hem of her ankle-length sari, hurried along the path with the rest of the villagers.

Drupadi felt himself irresistibly drawn in the same direction. Indeed, he was unable to stay away. Seven or eight
men in the ragged little group were shoving Patel ahead of
them on their way into Magadi. When the villagers saw
him, a hoarse shout of triumph echoed and reechoed over
the mountainside.

Drupadi hung back for a time, but when it was apparent
that nobody was paying any attention to him—not even his
father—he pushed through the crowd until he could see his
friend. Fright glittered in Patel's black eyes like the flames
of a campfire on a dark night. Patel's gaunt, hollowed
cheeks were pasty and his mouth was expressionless. Nala
was nearby, anger and sorrow mingling bitterly in his harsh,
weathered features, like the mixing of bitter herbs. And so
was Sati, the boy's mother. She made no sound but hot tears
coursed down her cheeks.

Drupadi tried to swallow, but could not. It would be the
same with his mother if they should find out what he had
done. She would not protest. The women of their people did
not; it was not their way. But she would mourn both for her
son and for the terrible thing he did. That would make it
even more difficult for him to bear.

9

Patel Is Punished

Sacuni held up his hand to quiet the restless villagers.

"We will hear the matter in the morning," he announced.

There was grumbling by those who wanted to settle the matter at once, but the village leader had spoken. There was none to stand against him.

Patel was taken to the guesthouse to spend the night and Sacuni posted guards around it. "This time," he explained, "Patel will not escape from us. This time we will learn the truth and exact a punishment that will satisfy the gods."

Drupadi quavered. This, too, had been his doing. If they learned anything at all the council would have a lot against him.

But the people acted as though he wasn't even there. A faint beam of hope began to glimmer within. Maybe Kittu had kept the information about him to himself after all! Maybe he had told no one!

At home after the evening meal it seemed that it must be so. His father was still talking about the wonderful thing that Kittu had done, savoring every detail as though it was some tasty morsel.

"Drupadi would like to hear how you found this—this former friend of his, my son," their father said. "Tell him how you found Patel."

91

Kittu lowered his gaze modestly. "It was nothing, my father."

That pleased Mukerji even more. "It may seem to be nothing to you," he beamed, "but now the gods will allow us to kill the tiger or drive him away. There will be no more shame for our village. We need no longer fear the vengeance of the gods."

He waited for his oldest son to begin.

"Tell him!" he ordered. "Tell all of us. I would hear it once more."

Pride swelled in Kittu's chest and a faint note of triumph crept into his voice. "I took the goats up on the mountain to graze, the way I always do when you are not with them, Drupadi."

The younger boy gulped wordlessly.

"Go on," their father said.

"And I heard this noise behind me, only it came from higher on the slope."

"Yes?" Mukerji leaned forward, tasting each word, savoring each hesitant phrase.

"I turned and saw Patel standing there. He ducked out of sight as quickly as he could, but I remembered a cave I found near there a long while ago and I figured Patel was hiding there."

"So you pretended not to see him so you wouldn't frighten him away. Is it not so?" Mukerji prompted.

"It is so, my father. And I left the goats where they were and hurried home to tell you."

Their father's smile was broad. "Is it not a fine older brother you have, Drupadi?" he asked proudly. "Is he not a delight to all of us?"

Drupadi cringed, but he had to speak. He had to make it

sound as though he was in agreement with them, that he, too, was glad Patel had been caught.

"I have two fine sons," Mukerji boasted. "The kind of sons who make a man's heart warm within him and give him pride before the elders in the village. It is good to have sons such as mine."

Drupadi's gaze lowered. What would his father say— what would he do if he knew the truth?

The next day all the men in the village and many of the women gathered in the marketplace when Patel was brought out. Drupadi was there, but he hung back in the long, deep shadow of a nearby hut. By this time he was convinced that if Kittu knew anything about his part in the matter he was not going to mention it. Now Patel was the only one who could give him away.

He waited breathlessly.

Sacuni told the charge against Patel. And Mukerji and two others, well respected in Magadi, related what had happened as the result.

"Now," Sacuni said, peering relentlessly into Patel's wavering gaze, "what do you have to say? Do you walk with this new God or not?"

Patel hesitated. He could no longer look into the angered face of the village leader, but was intently studying the ground at his feet.

"Patel!" his father rasped. "Tell them! Tell them the truth that you are not following the paths of the teacher and his new God! Tell them that you still worship in the way of our people!"

The boy's head rose almost reluctantly until he looked directly into his father's tortured gaze.

"But that would not be true, my father," he said clearly.

Astonishment rippled through the crowd, kindling anger

as it swept over the people. "Did you hear that?" they were muttering. "It is no wonder the gods sent the tiger to exact vengeance. It is a marvel they did not destroy us all."

"My son!" Nala cried in rage and frustration. "You told me you were giving up this strange God! You said you were coming back to the ways of our village. You promised to go with us to sacrifice the next time we went to the Temple of Rocks!"

"That was only because I was afraid." As Patel spoke his voice grew stronger. "And that was also why I ran away. My heart wanted to stay and speak the truth before the village elders, but my feet were weak and cowardly."

"No!" The word exploded from his father's lips. "Something has stolen your mind. You do not know what you are saying!"

"But I do know what I am saying, my father. I am saying that this Jesus the teacher has been telling us about is the true God. He—"

A shout went up.

"Enough!" Mukerji cried. "We have heard enough! Patel must stop before the gods get so angry they destroy us all!"

He continued sounding the cry, and others took it up until the village rang with it. Patel stood there calmly, waiting. At first he tried to make himself heard, but the shouting overpowered everything he tried to say. It cut off the words at his lips as though they had never been spoken. As hard as he tried, they would not let him continue.

A sudden strength-stealing numbness took hold of Drupadi. He had been afraid of what would happen. Now Patel had done just as he feared he would. He stood before all of Magadi and let the people know that he no longer put his trust in their old gods. He told them he was going the Jesus-way. He was still afraid. Drupadi could read the fear in his eyes. But there was something there he had never seen before—something he could not understand.

His mother touched him on the arm. "Come, my son," she whispered gently. "Let us go now."

Gratefully he followed her away from the crowd.

"Wh-what do you think they will do to him?" he murmured when they were on the path outside their hut. He dared to talk with his mother about such things because her lips would be sealed. And he had to do something to still the wild raging deep within him.

"To Patel?" she asked innocently, as though he could have been talking about anyone else.

"Will they stone him?"

She paused. "That I do not know, Drupadi. Maybe. Maybe no."

"Or do you think they might rob him of his mind?" This he had never seen, but he had heard the old ones talk about it, a punishment so severe that the person's mind was taken from him.

Again she could not answer with certainty. "If the punishment is given out by the council," she said, "no one can tell what they will do. The elders are frightened and very angry for this thing Patel has done. But Nala would probably be more gentle—more merciful. He is not the violent man some are."

Drupadi was caught in the web of his own thoughts. She was talking about his father, he knew. There was none in Magadi who was more stern and violent than his father, Mukerji. Still, he could not have his mother believe that this God the teacher talked about was unworthy to be worshiped.

"But, my mother, it is not bad that the teacher says, it is

good. He speaks of this new God, but in doing so he speaks of truth and living again—not as an animal or bird or a snake, but as people in a place called heaven. It brings joy just to listen."

He stopped suddenly, aware that he had pulled back the curtain to expose more of his heart than he should have, even to his mother.

Her gaze met his tenderly. "I, too, have felt the warmth of the teacher's words," she whispered. "And I have longed to know more about this God, myself. But we dare not listen to such things, my son. Your father is a good man, but he is so strong against those who would leave the old ways that there is no knowing what he would do if he were to learn that someone in his family was going off after this strange new God."

She trembled slightly. Her smile vanished and for an instant the lights in her eyes died. It was as though a cloud moved quickly across the face of the sun, leaving all bleak and cold and dark.

She looked down at Drupadi. "Promise me that you will never be so foolish as Patel was this morning, my son."

"You don't have to worry about me," he blurted fervently. "I'm not going to get the whole village against me."

She nodded thoughtfully, and for a time it appeared that she was going to speak once more, but she did not.

Mukerji and Kittu came back to the hut before long, triumphant but still loud in their anger at Patel.

"It is up to Nala to punish him in a way that is just," their father announced, "or the council will do it for him."

"Do you think they will steal his mind the way they used to do?" Kittu asked almost hopefully.

"Who can tell what punishment Nala will give him?" Scorn curled Mukerji's lips and the words knifed their way into Drupadi's heart. "I would show a son of mine! He would not make the people laugh at me and thrust out the lip, and still go unpunished. But Nala! He is Nala, the weak! The council might have to do his punishing for him."

He paused, slitted eyes fixed on first one of his sons and then the other.

"They would not have to punish Patel for me if he were my son. This I can tell you all! I would do it with my own two hands!"

Drupadi cringed. In some men such talk would be boasting that lacked meaning. Not so with his father. Drupadi knew too well that he meant everything exactly as he said. Mukerji did not joke. Nor did he make empty words about what he would do.

When Drupadi went to bed, however, it was not his father's bitter warning that he thought about. Instead, Patel's firm voice was resounding in his ears. His friend was so sure of what he believed. So positive that it was worth facing the council and his angry father—that it was the way a person should live in spite of all the punishment that might be given to him because of it.

Drupadi turned restlessly. If only he wasn't so afraid! But he could never be like Patel. He didn't have the strength and the courage to go the Jesus-way.

The following afternoon Mukerji came home with news of Patel.

"He is a stubborn boy and a shame to the honorable name of his father." He spit contemptuously. "I would rather have all of my sons dead than to see one of them turn on his family and the old ways of our people."

"What did Nala do to Patel?" their mother asked, glancing quickly at Drupadi.

Mukerji hunkered down against the wall on the hard dirt floor. "He beat him three times with a leather whip," he said, "in order to get him to take back his belief in this new God."

"And he did?" Drupadi asked hopefully.

The corners of his father's mouth twitched. "He is too stubborn for that! He is a worthless, lying son. Nala would be better off without him."

Drupadi caught his breath. He hadn't intended to. It was just that he was so overwrought, so upset by what had happened, that he was no longer as careful as he should be. His father caught his concern.

"You do not have feelings for this—this contrary son of Nala's." The words blistered his lips.

"It is not that," the boy protested defensively. "It is only that I—I—"

"If you were like Nala's son I would have no further use for you. I would not care if you lived or died."

"Drupadi is not like Nala's son," their mother said quietly. "He is a dutiful boy, mindful of the good name of his parents."

Mukerji was not so sure. "Kittu I trust. Of Drupadi, I am no longer so sure." He turned once more from his wife to his second-born son. "You say strange things, Drupadi. Things I have difficulty in understanding. You would not go the way Patel has gone, would you?" he demanded. "You would not follow his footsteps, would you?"

"I do as Patel has?" Drupadi summoned all his courage and laughed. "No one in the village would *dare* to do so after what has happened."

Mukerji considered that briefly. "It is so," he said. "And Patel will no longer be here in Magadi upsetting the villagers with his talking."

"What will Nala do with him?" their mother persisted gently.

"He beat him forty-five stripes with the whip, and when he would not turn back to our religion he asked the council to send Patel to the village of his relatives far from here. There is no teacher there to twist his mind or cause trouble for anyone else." His mouth hardened. "It was too easy for him, but the council decided that would have to be between the gods and Nala—that, as far as we are concerned, he is gone. And that will be enough to remove the punishment from Magadi."

Drupadi tried not to show his relief. It had, indeed, been most easy for Patel. The cuts on his back from the whip would heal and, as long as he didn't try to change anyone over to his new God, he would probably be treated the same as anyone else where he was going. At the moment the fact that Patel had not been seriously hurt or killed was good enough news for him.

It was some time before his father spoke again. "The council decided they will punish the ones who are responsible for what happened," Mukerji continued. "It was decided that we will take action against Sahib Conway and his son since they are the ones who caused the trouble with Patel. They should have to suffer for it!"

It was all Drupadi could to do keep silent, but he had to. He dared not speak and reveal the way he felt.

"There is more talk of this teacher's lessons in the village than any of us supposed," the boy's father continued. "People are being swayed by the things he is saying. They are believing what he says—or so it seems."

Drupadi wanted to demand his father to explain why he thought this development was so terrible. But this he could not do. Few dared to stand up to the fiery Mukerji, least of all his second-born son.

"They are saying in the village that Sahib Conway tried to talk a man into killing a sacred cow against his faith in order to give food to his family." Horror tinged Mukerji's voice at the thought that anyone could dare to voice such blasphemy. "And they are saying he killed a sacred cobra."

Drupadi studied his father's harsh face. He wanted to speak boldly, to ask the older man just who had said such things against the white teacher and his son. He wanted to go on to ask him what he knew about this Jesus he condemned so bitterly. But he did not. How could he when his father's anger could explode at any instant and destroy him at the same time?

"It is decided," Mukerji continued triumphantly. "When they come back they will be stoned."

Stoned! Drupadi all but gasped aloud. He had seen one stoning in the village. He had seen the wild anger of the crowd and heard the man's desperate pleading for mercy. He had seen the twisted, broken body when, fury spent, the crowd dispersed. He had not been there when the man died, but his older brother, Kittu, had, or so he said. And Drupadi had seen the grave himself!

10

Drupadi Decides

Drupadi did not know all that his father said that night, nor what he answered in return. But there were more bitter words against the teacher and his son—words so ugly that Drupadi's inner being reeled under them. He wanted to stop his ears with both hands to shut out the angry flow.

The teacher was an evil man, his father repeated, who deserved all the villagers would do to him when he returned. He had robbed Nala of his oldest son and brought the curse of the tiger to Magadi. Stoning was the only punishment for him.

And the younger one? It was unfortunate about him, Mukerji said. He did not like to think about stoning one so young, but there were times when the child had to suffer for the sins of the father.

Stoning did not always end in death, Drupadi realized as he sat there. Although it was bad enough, at best. There were those who were stoned and still lived. But for Sahib Conway, he knew they would not stop once the stoning began until the life had been beaten out of him. The men were too frightened and angry even to consider mercy. And it would be the same for Jack, who had done nothing to hurt anyone.

Perhaps this God the teacher talked about would protect him and his son. Surely those two would be worthy of His help, if any were.

But, even as Drupadi considered the possibility, doubt crept in. The new God had not kept Nala from beating Patel and sending him away. How could Drupadi expect Him to keep the teacher and his son from being stoned?

It might be like Patel said. Perhaps this God would give them strength and courage to take the stoning so the people of the village would see how much the teacher and his son loved Him.

But if something happened to the sahib, who would come to tell the people about the Jesus-way and going to heaven? Who would explain from the Book to them until their hearts burned with love for this One who loved them so much that He died to save them?

Drupadi jerked a quick breath into his lungs. The teacher and Jack meant much to him, it was true, and he ached for them as though he was being stoned himself. But suddenly he realized it was not for them that he was so troubled. It was for himself and the others in the village. There would be no one else to tell them about this new God if the teacher were stoned.

Drupadi still pondered the matter as he lay sleeplessly on his pad that night. There had to be something he could do to stop this terrible thing. But what? How could he stop it when all the village was against them? How could he make the men leave the sahib and Jack alone when he could not even stop Kittu from knocking him around?

Whether the teacher had done the things his father accused him of, Drupadi did not know. And, after listening to the sahib's talk of Jesus, he was not even sure whether it would be wrong to kill a sacred cow or cobra. The holy

Book could not forbid such things or the teacher would have told them.

He lay there quietly, a sudden wonder filling him. All those days and weeks he had been fighting against this God the teacher told about—this new God Patel was following. He had fought against the pain that lashed him as the teacher told that each person was a sinner and would have to pay the penalty for his sin. He had fought against the pleading of his heart to let this Jesus wipe away his sin and make him so he could go to heaven.

Now all the fighting against the things the teacher said was over. Both his mind and his heart saw that this was the way he should walk—that this new God was the One he was going to follow, even as Patel did.

A great peace swept over him. He began to understand something of how his friend felt and how he could stand against the council. He didn't think he had the courage to do so brave a thing, but he felt a new strength within him—a strength that was beyond his own.

If only he could do something to help the teacher and his son! If only there was some way to stop the stoning! Anguish surged within him.

The teacher spoke often about praying. But how could he pray to so great a God? He had never done anything for Him. Still, Patel had never done anything for Him either as far as he knew. And he said he prayed. Drupadi could not quite understand that, but there was no one else to whom he could turn. Patel was gone, and he could not even mention it to Kittu, so he talked to God about it.

The answer was so simple he smiled inwardly as it came and that same warm glow flowed over him. He could not stop his father and Sacuni from stoning the teacher and his son if they came to Magadi, but he could see that they did not come. It was as easy as that.

He didn't know why he hadn't thought of it before. It was not too far to the village where they lived. It was only over the mountain pass and halfway down the other side, much nearer the top of the ridge than Magadi. He could make it easily and get back while it was still dark and all the village slept.

Cautiously Drupadi slipped off the pad and past the sleeping Kittu. He crept to the window and peered out. But the moon was already far spent and in two hours it would begin to get light. There was no chance of making it safely back before dawn awakened the village.

At first the numbing ache rushed back to choke off his breath and set his stomach trembling. To know what to do and still not be able to do it was worse than having no plan at all.

Then relief flooded over him. There was no need to be in such haste. The teacher and Jack had only left Magadi the day before. They would not be coming back for almost a week. It would be better to wait until everything was right —until he was sure of success.

Carefully Drupadi worked out his plan. He would go to bed at the usual time, shortly after dark. Perhaps he might even go to bed a bit earlier than usual if he could do so without having his father or Kittu suspect something. Then, when everyone else in the village was sleeping, he would slip out of the house and run up the mountain and over the pass to the village where the teacher and his son made their home. He could warn them against returning to Magadi and get the sahib to bring him back most of the way in his jeep.

But there was the tiger! Drupadi had forgotten all about

the tiger in his concern for the sahib. Would the dreaded *shere* be down along the stream or up on the mountainside? Would the great beast be waiting to pounce on him somewhere along the road? His tongue clung dryly to the roof of his mouth and he was weak and sick inside. He did not have to fear the vengeance of the *shere,* he told himself. He was a follower of Jesus now. Yet he had to keep reminding himself of that.

His eyes were still open when daylight came and the others began to stir. He got up and talked with his mother, trying to mask his apprehension.

After breakfast Kittu wanted him to go up the mountain with him. "We won't be long," he said.

Drupadi kept his gaze lowered. His older brother was clever. He might read the concern and excitement and fear in his black eyes and pry his plan from him. Such things had happened before.

"I've got something else to do," he replied.

"I want to show you the cave Patel was hiding in."

Drupadi did not want to look at Kittu but he could not help it. His head came up and he searched his brother's eyes, curiously.

"I don't care to see it."

"What kind of a friend is that?"

Mealtime talk that evening was again of the teacher and his son. Mukerji repeated all that he had said before, enlarging on it maliciously. He told of new things the sahib had done to be worthy of stoning.

Drupadi could not allow himself to look into his father's face. He wanted to shout in protest and denial—to tell his father that all these things were not true and that the only thing the teacher had done was to tell the people of Jesus who loved them so much that He gave His life for them. But he dared not. It would only cause trouble for him and make it impossible for him to help the teacher. So he closed his ears against his father's railing. He did not trust himself to speak. He did not even trust himself to look at them.

Drupadi had planned on making the trip over the mountain the next night or the next; at the first opportunity he had to get away without being caught. But there was no chance early in the period. Kittu was up prowling about, or tossing so restlessly Drupadi could not be sure if he was asleep or not. At first the younger brother was content to wait, but as the number of nights dwindled until the teacher and his son were due to come back to Magadi his panic grew. Then one of the infrequent travelers from across the mountain pass to their village came with word that the sahib and his son would be returning to Magadi the next day.

"He asked me to tell you," the peddler said, "in case you want to go out after the tiger while he's here."

Mukerji's eyes gleamed evilly. "That was thoughtful of him."

Drupadi's mind reeled. The teacher and his son would be coming the next day! That meant he had to go over the mountain that night to warn them or let them come and be stoned. The sahib would have his rifle along but Drupadi knew he would never use it, not even to save his own life. Actually, it would be in its leather case in the back of the jeep. He wouldn't be able to get at it even if he would use it. He had to go and warn them. He was the only hope they had!

When he worked out his plan it had seemed easy enough, but now that he had to put it into being it was something else. His father was obstacle enough, but his brother was the one he really feared. Kittu was so suspicious and so cunning that there was no knowing what he would do.

At first Drupadi thought he would go to bed that night as soon as they finished eating, so he could get some rest before making the hurried trip over the mountain pass. But even that might cause Kittu to guess what he was about. He had to wait, to do everything as nearly the way he did on other nights as possible. Any change, however slight, made his plan more risky.

As they sat in the house after the evening meal Mukerji again delighted himself with the thought that the teacher was coming sooner than expected.

"The gods have decided they can't wait for vengeance so they're sending him to us now." He licked the food from his fingers and smacked his lips. "It will be a good day for Magadi, my sons," he continued. "This will be a day the tellers of stories will relate to your children and to your children's children."

Drupadi flinched. It was all he could do to remain quiet.

He waited until the usual time to lie down on his mat, but not to sleep. He was too excited—too frightened for that. He lay there in silence, eyes closed, listening for the regular breathing that would indicate the others were asleep. Usually they quieted shortly after going to bed, but not this time. One of the little ones fussed and their mother was up with her. Then their father remembered something he had to talk over with Sacuni. Drupadi was sure it had something to do with the stoning they planned. And so he was up and outside for a time.

At last Drupadi was sure that all was safe. Even after everything was still, he waited briefly. Then he got to his feet and edged off the pad, moving as noiselessly as a cobra slithered through the grass. No one could have heard him. That was sure. But Kittu stirred and opened his eyes.

At the first whisper of movement, Drupadi froze, one foot lifted off the hard dirt floor. For a brief instant he did not move at all. Then, slowly, his head was turned until his eyes met those of his older brother.

Terror spasmed Drupadi's slight young body. Somehow Kittu knew what he was about to do.

Kittu knew!

For the space of one agonizing heartbeat Drupadi stood over his older brother, uncertainty and terror mingling in his dark young features. He had never seen Kittu this way before. There was no anger in his stare. No arrogance. Only a desperate, wordless pleading.

Drupadi was paralyzed. He could not move. He could not even speak. And Kittu was the same. Only his desperate gaze gave voice.

"No, Drupadi!" his black eyes shouted. "Don't go! Don't risk our father's anger!"

But Kittu did not know about the burning in his heart, about the weakness that surged over him when he thought of life in Magadi without the sahib's visits to tell them about God. He had to go! It was the only way the teacher and his son could be spared. It was the only way the people in the village could hear more of this new God who brought such gladness to him.

Mutely his own eyes pleaded with Kittu for silence, for a chance to slip out of the hut and do this thing he had to do. Indecision flickered in his brother's gaze. Drupadi knew that he was wavering.

Kittu, too, had heard the teacher. He, too, had felt the emptiness of his life and the awfulness of the things that he had done—the sin in his life, as his brother called it. He,

too, felt the guilt of this new God upon him, and the terrible longing to follow in the Jesus-way.

His brother had never mentioned these things to Drupadi. Actually, he would have denied that he had ever heard them, with a curse and a cuff on the side of Drupadi's head. But Drupadi knew his older brother well, even as Kittu knew him. Only fear of their father and the villagers kept him from doing what Patel and Drupadi had done in deciding to walk the paths of Jesus.

Kittu's hesitance, the chance that he might betray him, brought sweat to Drupadi's forehead and stole his courage, leaving his knees rubbery and trembling.

He knew the teacher and his son would pray at a time like this, but he knew so little of praying to the God who could answer him that he was uncertain even how to begin. Yet a desperate, silent cry for help went up as he stood there—a cry he could not put into words.

He dare not wait! There was no time for that! Whatever he did had to be done. He had to go now—this very moment—or let the teacher and his son come back to Magadi and be stoned.

Stealthily he turned and picked his way to the door and out into the chill mountain air. Half a second passed while he stood there hesitantly, peering into the moonless night and weighing the cost. Could he go through with it? Did he dare to try?

Kittu answered the question for him—answered it with a shrill cry that all but marbleized him where he stood.

"My father!" Kittu shouted in a voice loud enough to waken half the village. "My father! Drupadi has gone! He has run away to the teacher across the mountain!"

11

Villagers Pursue

DRUPADI FROZE, even as he had frozen when he first saw the pug marks of the tiger on the bank of the stream. He knew well enough what would happen next; in an instant the entire village would be awake. Men would be running after him, their torches punching holes in the darkness, searching out the likely places to hide. He had to run now—run like the *chital,* the fleet-footed little axis deer—run until his heart was close to bursting and his lungs were aflame.

The paralysis ebbed as swiftly as it came and Drupadi was able to move once more. Frantically he scurried out of the village and up the steep mountain slope. The narrow, twisting road wound its way leisurely up the mountain. It was an easy road to travel, and at first he started up it instinctively because it was the way everyone going up the mountain used. It was the way the teacher and Jack always came in their jeep. But suddenly Drupadi realized that he dared not use it. The road was the place the men would search first. And, whatever happened, he could not allow himself to be caught.

It was cold on the steep mountain slope and a sharp wind was whining out of the west—the kind of wind that set the people to shivering in their drafty, unheated huts.

Drupadi's feet were bare, and the stones cut and bruised

them as he scrambled higher and higher. Fortunately he knew every foot of the steep slope, every crevice, every great, jagged boulder behind which to hide.

He had almost delayed too long back at the house. He had heard the wild shouts of alarm spread through the village when he skittered past the last hut and left the road. Already the men of Magadi were up and looking for him. Glancing over his shoulder, he could see the flare of their torches as they rushed from one hut to the other. For a moment he could not figure out what they were doing. Then he realized that they must think he was still in the village, that perhaps he had gone into the home of one of his friends in a desperate attempt to hide.

He was thankful for that. It gave him yet another precious minute or two to widen the gap between himself and his would-be captors.

It wasn't long until the pattern in the village changed. Two torches were moving rapidly up the narrow road that led across the mountain pass. That meant Sacuni had sent two men on bicycles up the road to be sure he wouldn't be able to cross the ridge to the other side.

In a terrifying instant their plan lay nakedly before him. The two men would drive him upward slowly, relentlessly, not caring at all whether they found him during the darkness, but only that they kept him moving ahead of them. Sooner or later daylight would chase away the last hiding place and he would be trapped against the uncrossable spine of the mountain. Then they would have him.

As he came to understand how they planned to capture him, his legs turned to stone and his courage to that of a jackal. He came to a halt and sagged against a boulder. In agony his lungs fought against the iron bands of exhaustion that tightened about his chest.

He had to push on, higher and higher and higher. Stopping would mean that he would be caught. And yet it was only postponing what was sure to happen. If only there was some other way over the mountain other than the pass. If only he— He straightened suddenly. Why hadn't he thought of it before? Why hadn't he thought about going over the ridge the way Kittu had shown him?

But that had been a long time ago, before his feet were sure and his will was strong enough to go so high among the rocks where a single slip would have meant a fall that would crush out his life. He and Kittu had been gathering firewood on the mountain when suddenly his older brother asked if he wanted to see how brave he was. Kittu swore him to secrecy and took him up to the forbidding jumble of boulders and cliffs that made up the spine of the ridge.

"I cannot go there, Kittu!" he remembered saying with awe. "Nobody could."

"Watch!" And his older brother had laughed exultantly.

Up and up Kittu had climbed with the ease of a mountain goat until at last he stood on the very spine of the range.

"From here I can see Chalama!" he had shouted.

Drupadi's admiration and pride for his older brother had increased immeasurably at that moment.

Drupadi had always been a little afraid of the place, so he had not been back there since. He was not sure now that he would be able to locate it—especially in the dark. The way up had been almost impossible to see until they were almost upon it. He recalled that.

And if he wasn't able to find it? What then? The chill bit into him savagely. It would not be easy to remember the landmarks, although they seemed easy enough for his brother to follow.

The place was on the other side of the road—far on the

other side. What if the villagers saw him as he crossed it? What if he got lost in the darkness? What if—

If only he could have talked Kittu into going with him. He must have been there often. He would have led him unerringly to the path. Kittu would have been able to guide them up the steep cliffs even in the dark. If Kittu were along now they would probably have made their way over the mountain ridge and have been hurrying down the opposite slope in the direction of Chalama.

But he did not have Kittu with him. He was alone. Alone! And if he was going to find the way to the other side he was going to have to hurry. Every minute of delay brought the villagers nearer and cut his chance of escaping.

Drupadi had been climbing almost straight up the mountain since first leaving Magadi, drawing away from the relentless searching of the villagers as quickly as possible. Now, however, he had to change directions and move parallel to them, watching the torches draw closer and closer.

The nearer the men got to him, the more danger there was that he might make a slip that would mean his capture. The villagers who were following him had also been born and raised on the mountain. They, too, knew most of its secrets. Their ears were as sharp and as sensitive as the nose of a deer. Their eyes like the eyes of the tiger, piercing the darkness. The closer they got to him, the more serious his position became.

Drupadi jerked to a halt! There was something out in the darkness to his right! Something that moved with stealthy cunning so quietly he could not be entirely sure he had heard anything at all. He crouched motionless, waiting!

At first he thought of Kittu. Maybe his brother was moving about the mountain slope without a torch, hoping to stumble onto him in the darkness. But that could not be, he reasoned. Even one who knew the mountain as well as his older brother would not be able to move so quietly nor see in the black of the night.

As he waited a small pebble dislodged from its resting place and rolled down a few feet with hushed, rattling sounds.

Drupadi's blood iced! The tiger!

The *shere* was being forced up the mountain ahead of the villagers, frightened by the noise and the flames of the torches.

Fear gripped him forcibly and he fought against it.

He had to wait, as hard as that was, until the tiger got a short distance away from him. The big animal was on the move now. He should keep going. He was probably so concerned about the confusion of noise and fire that he didn't even know Drupadi was near.

All the boy had to do was to wait for a while. But he could not wait too long or the men coming up the mountain would capture him.

Grimly he forced his attention to the business at hand. There was no time now for fear. He had to give the tiger time to get a safe distance away from him, but at the same time he had to watch the searchers warily to be sure they did not get close enough to hear or see him. Equally important, he had to keep pressing until he found the way to the mountaintop. He had to find it while the protective cloak of darkness was still about him. And to do so, he would have to cut across the road, traveling the same direction the tiger had gone.

He had not moved more than a hundred yards when there was a low, ominous growl somewhere just ahead. He froze suddenly. A cry went up! A wild, exultant, triumphant cry!

"Eeeiye!"

It was swallowed by a wild roar of pain.

The cry went up again, louder this time. Others were shouting too as they ran in the direction of the sounds.

Drupadi shuddered. He knew what had happened. In the dark of the night a spear-bearing villager had come upon the ugly, evil *shere* and managed a fatal blow.

For an instant or two he did not move, transfixed by the unexpected destruction of the vicious man-eater. Briefly relief swept over him. Magadi was free of the curse of the tiger; the people would not have to worry about him again.

Then a shout went up in the darkness not far away. The men were starting to move again, leaving the tiger's carcass and continuing the search for him.

He hurried upward, angling in the direction of the path. The nearer he got to it, the more his apprehension grew. Half a dozen men had converged upon it, making their way painstakingly through the boulders on either side. They were probing each hiding place as they came to it, holding their torches high to chase away any protective shadows.

12

Drupadi Escapes

D<small>RUPADI WAS A SCANT</small> fifty paces
ahead of the searchers when he reached the road. For an
anxious moment he paused, staring fearfully down at them.
They were close enough so the light of their torches etched
their angered faces in sharp relief. Drupadi shuddered and
then scampered across the road.

Once he was on the other side, the distance between
himself and the men of Magadi began to increase. The
villagers nearest the trail pushed faster, spurred on appar-
ently by the belief that he would try to parallel the road
even though he dare not use it. The others had more ground
to cover and did so slowly. The lights from their torches
moved back and forth, only inching upward. Even so, they
were drawing dangerously close to him—so close he almost
feared to breathe.

Let him stumble and fall noisily or have a bit of trouble
locating the route to the top and across to the other side and
they would have him. That realization drove him on in
desperation.

His feet, bruised and bleeding, were only stubs that had
long since ceased to register pain. Each breath was an
effort. His flaming lungs cried out for him to stop and end
the agony. Each throbbing muscle pleaded for relief. It
would be so easy, so very easy to crouch behind a boulder
and wait for them to find him.

Surely the punishment that would be his would not be worse than the torture he was putting himself through. Perhaps his father would do nothing at all to him if he told the elders he would turn his back on the teacher and promise that he would worship the gods of their people. That was what his father would want. That and the opportunity to stone this one who had come to the village with news of this new God.

But how could Drupadi say he would go back to the ways of his father? He had given his heart and his life to the white teacher's God.

And the stoning! If he did not go on, the sahib and Jack would come over the mountain and be stoned by the villagers! He could not allow that to happen! Not as long as he could struggle upward! Not as long as he could keep out of the grasp of the desperate villagers. Grimly Drupadi forced himself on and up as rapidly as he could climb.

The first gray streak of dawn lay along the eastern horizon. It was only a sliver of light at first, peeking above the mountaintop—so faint that it made no impression at all on the darkness. But it gave warning that the night was all but spent, that daybreak was practically upon them, and soon the hiding shadow of darkness would disappear.

Summoning strength he did not know he had, Drupadi broke into a run. He could make out the shapes of the boulders now, and the torches below seemed to be fading in intensity. But that was only because the darkness was lessening. It also meant that he had to be more careful than ever lest he be seen.

How had Kittu located the place? he asked himself. There was the queerly shaped boulder that looked as though someone had balanced it on a tiny corner and a breath of air would be enough to send it toppling. And, higher, there had been the slice in the granite cliff, an opening a little wider than a man's shoulders and almost perpendicular. That had been the way up for the first fifty feet. If he could—

There were other signs he remembered as he went along —signs that only one born to the mountains would have noted and stored away in the corners of his mind. At last, as dawn was full upon them, he saw the place.

Joy died an icy death in his heart. There was the narrow split in the ledge that led to the top of the rocky spine and down the other side. There also was Kittu sitting, cross-legged, with his back against the cliff. While Drupadi crouched behind a boulder, he could hear the men below shouting to one another.

He was trapped! For a moment or two he crouched there in the dull gray of early morning. His breath came in thin, shallow gasps and his heartbeat was light and fluttery. The sweat on his forehead was dried by the chill wind. Narrowly he squinted at Kittu. His brother's eyes were closed and he dozed fitfully, head nodding.

For one brief instant Drupadi weighed the chance of sneaking past his brother while he slept. It was tempting, but it would be impossible, he knew. Kittu slept lightly. Drupadi had not even been able to get up from his pad at home without waking him. He wouldn't get half across the open space before Kittu would grab him.

Frantically he looked about. If there was just some place a hundred yards or so to one side or the other where he could climb the first fifty to one hundred feet he might have a chance of making his way back along the wall to Kittu's path without disturbing him.

To the left the cliff was sheer and smooth. Further to the right looked more promising. The wall was not so perpen-

dicular there, and there were cracks and fissures that might offer him places to dig in with his fingers and toes. But cracks like that, if they were deep and wide enough, would also be attractive hiding places for snakes. A shudder ran over his lithe body.

But he could not wait there any longer. Each passing minute gave the newborn sun time to chip away at the early morning haze, making his position all the more dangerous. Summoning what little courage he had left, he made his way along the slope to a stretch of cliff that appeared to be climbable. Moving his feet as quickly as the stalking tiger moved his paws, Drupadi crossed the rock-strewn ledge below the cliff. Kittu had not heard him. Indeed, he could not have heard him had he been four paces away because the gentle hush of breeze swallowed the little sound he made.

At the cliff Drupadi paused for an agonizing instant. How could he ever have thought the cliff could be climbed now? How could he hope to go up without disturbing Kittu or being seen by the men on the mountain below him? Doubts and fears churned in endless confusion in his heart.

But he could not linger here. Resolutely he reached, found a slight crack with his hand, and started up.

Drupadi had climbed before—for fun and of necessity. He knew how to claw his way up a steep rock wall, how to take advantage of every indentation, every tiny crack. But never had he climbed with such daring, such fierce determination.

He could not climb slowly for the risk of being seen was greater than the risk of falling. He could not put a hand or foot in a place that would be apt to send a rock clattering down the sheer granite cliff. That would alert Kittu and the others quicker than anything else. He had to move silently, rapidly, from hold to hold.

Plastered against the wall, he would be an easy target for the eyes of any of a half-dozen men when the last wisps of mist had burned away.

At last he had climbed as high as he could go without moving over toward Kittu. The rock face was perpendicular for a distance of twenty feet or so, then it slanted outward and upward for another one hundred and fifty feet. The only course was to inch along the cliff, half a step at a time, to the place almost directly above where Kittu had stationed himself. Once there he could climb upward again to the very spine of the mountain five hundred feet above. Then, and only then, would he be out of reach of the villagers. He knew they would not cross the mountain peak to get him.

The mist and haze were all but gone now that the sun was pushing above the mountains to the east. A few more minutes and anyone who chanced to look up would see him. He knew nothing at all of praying but, once more—in great desperation, his heart cried out to God for help.

The minutes dragged endlessly by as he inched along the sheer rock cliff until, at last, he was practically above Kittu.

He looked up and his heart almost burst for joy. Here he was! He had finally reached the top. The rest of the climb would be difficult but it would be fast. Even if someone saw him now and started after him, he knew that he would easily be able to get away.

He glanced down. Kittu was stretching now and looking anxiously about. Drupadi felt the pain stab deeply into him as his brother moved. Kittu had also heard the teacher. He, too, had been touched by the words he spoke. He, too, had felt the longing to take this Jesus as his own.

But he was afraid.

Again the joy and peace that came over Drupadi back home as he realized he was trusting his heart and his life to Jesus, engulfed his being. Whatever else happened to him, he knew that he was a follower of the teacher's God. He had confessed his sin and was trusting Jesus to save him from the terrible place called hell.

That was where Kittu was going unless he, too, decided to walk with the new God. The thought stopped Drupadi briefly. He clung to the cliff and looked down at his brother once more with longing.

If Kittu knew what Drupadi had done and what he was going to do, if he knew that he was sure to get away now, there was a chance that Kittu might join him.

Drupadi hesitated. If he went down to Kittu and talked with him once more, his brother might also go with him and become a follower of the God the teacher talked about. But then again, he might grab Drupadi by the arm and shout for the others. Then he remembered Patel and what had happened to him.

He shuddered. Uncertainly he clung there. He didn't know what Kittu would do, or what would happen to him or to the sahib and his son if Kittu cried out. Drupadi only knew that he had to talk with him once more, that he had to give him one more chance to become a Christian.

Hurriedly he made his way down to a spot some six or eight feet above where Kittu was sitting.

"Kittu!" he hissed. "My brother!"

The boy on the ground jerked erect, listening.

"Kittu!"

"Drupadi!" His voice was hushed and awestruck. "What are you doing here?"

"I came back to talk to you."

"But how did you get up there? I mean—" His voice trailed away.

"There is no time to talk of that now. Come! We must hurry!"

Questions gleamed in the older boy's eyes. "Where do you go?" he demanded. "To Chalama, the village of the teacher?"

Drupadi's dark eyes lighted briefly, hopefully. "To the village of the teacher, Kittu."

"But you cannot go there. Our father is angry and all the men of Magadi look for you."

"I know. I have spent the night on the mountain."

Silence hung tautly between them. At last Kittu was able to force out the words.

"Why have you come back, my brother," he demanded, "when you are on the way to safety?"

"You heard the teacher too," Drupadi whispered. After he spoke he jumped down lightly and stood beside his brother. "You will go with me?"

Horror leaped to Kittu's eyes. "Don't you know how angry the elders are?" he asked. "Don't you know they are going to stone the sahib and his son when they come back today? Don't you know what happens when someone does what you say and walks the way of the teacher's new God?" His voice broke. "Don't you remember Patel?"

Drupadi nodded wordlessly.

"Then why do you come back to ask such a thing of me?"

"It is for you, Kittu," he said earnestly. "I know you listened to the teacher too. I know the ache in your heart—the same ache that held me before I changed and became a follower of Jesus. I thought that maybe if you knew that I'd go with you—that we could both go together—that you would find courage to go along."

Kittu's anger flamed. "It is not for fear that I do not go with you to the teacher in Chalama, Drupadi," he said. "It is—" His voice choked and he could not finish. "Don't you know that all I have to do is to call out and the men will come running up and grab you, or stone you on the cliff until you fall?"

Drupadi's mouth went hot and dry. "I—I know."

"Don't you know that I am the one who woke up our father last night and caused the men to come after you?"

"I know," he acknowledged.

"And still you came back?"

"I thought maybe you would go with me, Kittu," he said in desperation. "I want you to follow this Jesus too."

Hurt kindled in his older brother's eyes and flamed there, but in a moment it mingled with fear.

"I—" He swallowed hard. "I—I dare not go, Drupadi. I dare not!"

"It is only the climb of a few minutes. The worst is over,

Kittu. Then you, too, will have this joy, this peace in the heart that belongs to those who walk the Jesus-way."

Anger flashed suddenly across the older boy's taut face as though he had already made up his mind. "Talk no more of it to me!" he rasped. "And go!"

"But, Kittu!"

"Go now! I will give you until you reach the ledge before I call to them. Stay and I shout at once!"

The finality in his voice left Drupadi no choice. He had to leave. He sprang to get his foot in the first hold and hurriedly worked his way upward. He did not look back but he knew that Kittu was still standing motionless, his eyes turned upward. His brother had been so close, so very close to going with him.

True to his word, Kittu waited until he reached the ledge. Then his cry went up, shrill and angry.

"Here he is! This way! Hurry! He's getting away!"

The very sound of it, although Drupadi knew it was coming, chilled the blood in his veins. Far below he heard the excited clatter of voices and the sounds of running feet. An instant later a rock, thrown by a villager, ricocheted off the granite cliff not a foot from his head.

"No!" he heard Kittu shout in desperation. "Don't do that!"

But that did not stop them. A rock hit him in the thigh and another on the shoulder, but already he was so high the force was spent. Their shouted threats and pleading drifted up to him as he climbed, but he gave no mind to them. It was almost as though he could not hear them.

Once on the jagged ridge of the mountain, he straightened and looked back. The men shook their fists at him and shouted, but Kittu waved. Drupadi raised his own arm in a silent good-bye to his brother.

He stood motionless, looking down at them. The tiger was gone; he would never be able to terrorize Magadi again. The slender boy was thankful for that.

Slowly he turned and made his way down the other side in the direction of Chalama. He would not see his parents or Kittu or the little ones for a long while. Indeed, he would not dare to go back until their hearts had softened toward Jesus. It would be a long while before the teacher, Sahib Conway, would be able to go back either. They might have to wait until some of the village elders who were the most opposed to the Jesus-way had died. There was an aching in his heart as he thought of that.

But there was joy too. He was a follower of this wonderful Jesus. He had given his heart and his life to Christ. He was no longer bound by fear and superstition. He did not have to be afraid of the spirits and all the taboos that made the lives of his people so miserable. His faith in Jesus made him free!

He thought back to his mother and that longing in her dark eyes. She, too, had been touched by the teacher's talk of Jesus. In her heart she might already be a follower—afraid to speak out for fear of his father, but guarding those things in her heart.

And Kittu! He knew from his wave that one day his brother would also gain the courage to cross the mountaintop to come and sit at the sahib's feet and hear more of Jesus. That would be a happy day! Just thinking of it brought a smile to his face.

Drupadi's downward pace quickened as he hurried to the village of Chalama and the teacher, Sahib Conway, and his son, Jack. It was a sad day, but at the same time it was the happiest and most wonderful day in all his life.

Glossary

Ardjuna	— Ard-june'-ah	— brother of Patel
Brahman	— Brah'-men	— highest caste in India
Chalama	— Sha-lah'-ma	— the village where Missionary Conway and his son live
Charpoy	— Char-poy'	— Indian bed. A wooden frame with heavy twine woven in 3 by 3-inch squares to serve as a mat or springs.
Chital	— Sh'-tall	— fleet-footed deer
Drona	— Droh'-nah	— an elder in the village of Magadi
Drupadi	— Drew-pad'-ee	— son of Mukerji and Khati
Kali	— Call'-ee	— four-armed black goddess of generation and destruction
Khati	— Kah'-tee	— mother of Drupadi and Kittu
Kittu	— Kit'-oo	— brother of Drupadi
Langur	— lung-goor'	— any of a subfamily of long, slender Asian monkeys
Machan	— May'-can	— platform in a tree. Used to hunt from
Magadi	— Mah-ga'-di	— the village where Drupadi lives
Mahout	— ma-howt'	— elephant handler
Mukerji	— Moo-cur'-gee	— father of Drupadi and Kittu
Nala	— Nah'-lah	— father of Patel and Ardjuna
Narada	— Nar-ah-dah'	— messenger of the spirits
Niagroda	— Ny-ah-grow'-dah	— a kind of tree
Patel	— Paw-tel'	— son of Nala and Sati
Sacuni	— Sah-coon'-nee	— an elder in the village of Magadi
Sahib	— Sa'-heb	— sir or mister. A designation of respect
Sati	— Sah'-tee	— mother of Patel and Ardjuna
Shere	— Share	— tiger
Tacsaca	— Talk-sak'-a	— king of the snakes in Hinduism